"You're too beautiful not to be kissed," Jack whispered, his voice husky with the same tension Lila felt with every breath. **"Especially on New Year's Eve."**

His hand slid to the nape of her neck as his mouth claimed hers in a series of teasing explorations. Lila found her reasoning powers melting with each light kiss he feathered across her lips. Each brief touch fanned a flame deep inside her, recalling the moonlit night when a stranger had kissed her, and seemed not to be a stranger at all.

In the way dusk slips into darkness, gentleness turned into passion, and memories into a startling present. Lila felt the muscles in his arms flex as he gathered her closer. She felt her own heart beating a new rhythm, and she heard his breath grow ragged and heavy as he kissed her deeper, longer, slower. She reached for him to steady her world, but instead she found the closeness of his body further disorienting. It had been too long, and he felt too good. . . .

WHAT ARE *LOVESWEPT* ROMANCES?

They are stories of true romance and touching emotion. We believe those two very important ingredients are constants in our highly sensual and very believable stories in the *LOVESWEPT* line. Our goal is to give you, the reader, stories of consistently high quality that may sometimes make you laugh, sometimes make you cry, but are always fresh and creative and contain many delightful surprises within their pages.

Most romance fans read an enormous number of books. Those they truly love, they keep. Others may be traded with friends and soon forgotten. We hope that each *LOVESWEPT* romance will be a treasure—a "keeper." We will always try to publish

*LOVE STORIES YOU'LL NEVER FORGET
BY AUTHORS YOU'LL ALWAYS REMEMBER*

The Editors

Loveswept ® 500

Glenna McReynolds
Moonlight and Shadows

BANTAM BOOKS

NEW YORK · TORONTO · LONDON · SYDNEY · AUCKLAND

To Patti—with love.

MOONLIGHT AND SHADOWS

A Bantam Book / October 1991

If you would be interested in receiving protective vinyl
covers for your Loveswept books, please write to this address
for information:

Loveswept
Bantam Books
P.O. Box 985
Hicksville, NY 11802

ISBN 0-553-44138-8

Published simultaneously in the United States and Canada

PRINTED IN THE UNITED STATES OF AMERICA

OPM   0 9 8 7 6 5 4 3 2 1

Prologue

The lady had more money than brains, Jack Hudson thought, and from the figures she'd given him, she was operating on a shoestring in the money department. He slowly shook his head behind her back, watching her paint with hand gestures her imaginary desires.

"Windows are the key," she said, "the very heart of what I want. Space." Lila Singer raised both arms to encompass the moon and the stars, as if the very heavens could be hers. "Lots and lots of space."

In a ten by twenty addition? Jack asked silently. She had to be kidding. Of course, at five foot two and—what? A hundred and five pounds?—she probably thought anything bigger than a breadbox had space.

A crisp September breeze blew through the cottonwood trees, and he shoved his hands deeper into his jacket pockets, hunching his shoulders against the chill. She had to be cold in her flimsy cotton dress.

The breeze kicked up into a true prairie wind, and he couldn't help but notice how the cotton molded around Lila Singer's hips and legs. Okay, so the lady has a great body, small but perfect, like one of those fairy queens he'd seen in a storybook once.

He exhaled a deep breath. He didn't have any business thinking about Lila Singer's body. She'd called him out to her house to look at a job, not her legs. Besides, he had a date that night, a blind date with a woman named Rachel. He didn't know what to expect, or why he'd let his supposedly best friend talk him into the guaranteed disaster. His stomach was in knots, which was the only reason he was standing in Lila Singer's cornfield. He didn't have time to take on another job, but he'd needed something to do besides pace his living room until eight o'clock. He shook his head again.

He could have stayed home, *should* have stayed home. He had lots to do. There was always his front porch to work on, or the back deck, and it was really time for him to finish plastering the main hall. Or he could have done what he usually did at night and worked in the garage until the wee hours. He had a new project, the biggest thing he'd ever tackled, a dream in his head he wanted to make happen.

"See those mountains over there?" The fairy queen with the crazy ideas pointed to the west as she glanced at him over her shoulder.

Jack nodded, returning his attention to the project at hand. The Rockies, fourteen thousand feet of Mother Earth's granite, were kind of hard to miss.

"When I'm in my office," she said, "I want to feel like they're sitting in my lap." She turned to face him, a serenely beautiful smile curving her mouth, and suddenly Jack saw her—really saw her—for the first time. He'd been talking with her for over a half an hour, inside the house and out, but he hadn't truly looked at her until that moment. She was gorgeous, her smile a gift of sweetness he felt spreading all through his body. But with the gift came a strong pang of guilt. She was trying so hard to explain what she wanted, and he was barely listening. He felt like a jerk, a jerk whose stomach was in knots.

Don't do it, Jack, he warned himself. Don't fall for a pretty lady with a smile sweeter than honey. You've got three other jobs lined up. Big jobs. Big houses. Big money. Inside work, Jack, and winter's coming on.

"Can you do it?" she asked. Even her voice had an ethereal quality, soft and breathy. And he hadn't noticed before, but her hair was like a cloud, a storm cloud of tumbling dark curls framing her face.

Her face . . . He studied the delicate, gamine-like curves; the wide, dark eyes; the little nose and the full mouth. Too full for his tastes, he quickly decided, recognizing the familiar sensation invading his mind. He wanted to kiss this woman. Why? he wondered, shaken by the realization. She wasn't his type.

Right, Jack. With a concentrated effort he shrugged off the strange urge to kiss Lila Singer.

"Mr. Hudson?" She looked up at him with those

liquid brown eyes, drawing his gaze to her thick lashes and the sable arch of her eyebrows, so in contrast with her blush-rose cheeks and creamy skin. A very sensual contrast, he mused, a mystery of genetics, a— "Will you take the job?"

"Yes," he heard himself answer as if from a long distance. Then he realized what he'd said and silently cursed. How had that happened?

"Wonderful." The bright warmth of her smile and the excitement in her voice slowly drew him in again. "When can you start?"

Jack struggled to organize dates, names, supplies, all the while staring at her face, her eyes, her mouth. Forcing a measure of clarity into his mind, he came up with only one possible, lousy answer. "I won't be doing the work myself. My partner, Dale Smith, will be out this weekend to look things over."

Smitty should be able to build one small but spacious addition without screwing it up, Jack assured himself. For five years the man had been a rock of stability, helping Hudson and Smith Construction grow into a reliable and lucrative company. But he was in the middle of a divorce and had the current attention span of a hyperactive seven-year-old, which Jack knew from personal childhood experience wasn't much.

"Well, you were recommended to me as the best," she said, "I'll look forward to seeing Mr. Smith on Saturday, then. Or will it be Sunday?"

"Saturday," Jack said with a confidence he hoped wasn't misplaced. He'd have to make damn sure Smitty didn't tie one on Friday night. "He'll look at the plans you bought, give you a formal estimate and show you catalogues from our window suppliers. Of course, if you already have windows picked out, we can order from anybody. But the people we deal with regularly give us a better price." He rattled on, liking the feeling of control conversation gave him. But he was running out of small talk. "And he'll bring the contracts for you to sign. Have you had anybody else out to look at the job?"

"No. I know that sounds silly." She laughed, an enchanting sound reminiscent of bells and chimes blowing in the wind. His brows drew together in confusion. What was it about this woman? "But you came *very* highly recommended. You did some work for my parents last year. Dad said you were more expensive than the other people, but he also said I'd get better work and better value dealing with you."

"That's always nice to hear." Maybe that was where the strange feeling was coming from, he mused. Maybe she looked like her mother and he thought he knew her. But even as the explanation crossed his mind, he discounted it. He wouldn't have forgotten his woman.

She said something polite, something he didn't bother to catch. Lord, she was pretty, standing there looking up at him with moonlight and shadows tangled in her hair. Lots of moonlight, more than he ever remembered seeing. He glanced at the glowing orange disk rising above the horizon. A full moon, he thought. A harvest moon. Maybe that explained the strange detachment he felt stealing over him, as if he were operating on two different planes, one very normal with all its everyday complications, and the other . . . different, peaceful, filled with a promise he hadn't known for many years.

His gaze drifted back from the heavens to the stars in her eyes. Wind swirled around the two of them, picking up the tawny fallen leaves and tossing them into the air. A few landed in her hair, hanging for a fleeting moment in the sable strands like a circlet of gold. How had he missed her beauty at first? And was it his imagination, or was she getting prettier with every passing moment? No answers came to his odd question until she took a step toward him.

His normal half told him she was walking back to the house. But the half of him mired in the moon's magic told him she was coming to him, and right then and there Jack Hudson did the craziest thing he'd ever done.

With the barest touch of his hand on her face, he stopped her, then bent forward from the waist, lower and lower, pulled like the tides to her too-full mouth. His lips grazed hers, softly at first, then with more pressure as her ripe sweetness blossomed under his mouth. She smelled of flowers and warm sunshine even in the cool darkness of the autumn night. Her lips parted, and he followed the path into a kiss of mystery.

Minutes later—or was it hours?—he lifted his head. Gentle arousal thrummed through his body. The wind ruffled her hair, and he stroked the silky strands, absently tucking them behind her ear.

"Thank you, Lila." His voice was husky, the smile on his face one of sheer contentment. Maybe later he'd feel foolish, but try as he might, he didn't feel foolish then. He felt whole. "Smitty will be around on Saturday."

Looking thoroughly dazed, she nodded. The action brought his fingers in contact with the velvety softness of her cheek. Unbidden by conscious thought, he bent his head once more and pressed a kiss to her brow. Then he turned and walked away.

Lila stared after him, struck dumb by the power of his kiss and her own startling response. The man had hardly spoken twenty words to her, and she was sure he hadn't heard twenty of hers. Then he up and kissed her? She should have slapped him, for crying out loud, not melted in his arms.

But she had melted. Why?

She touched her lips, and the warmth was still there. If she touched her cheek she knew she'd find warmth there, too, despite the chill tickling her skin.

The cab light in his truck came on when he opened the door, and in the seconds before it went off, he looked back at her, his clear gaze reaching across the night to hold her with intimacy and a disarming tenderness.

Disarming? Yes. She hadn't known he was going to kiss her until it had been far too late to think. His mouth had been so warm, wet, enticing, his tongue stroking hers in an erotic dance. Had she really touched his face, felt the day's growth of beard? Tunneled her fingers into his sandy brown hair, traced the lean angles of his face?

He was so tall, his body lanky and hard. She didn't like tall men, had decided as a teenager that she didn't want to spend her life looking at a man's chest instead of his face.

His face . . . Her memory conjured up the rough handsomeness of Jack Hudson's face, the feathery lines at the corners of his eyes, his sun-darkened skin, his silky eyebrows. Lord! Had she touched him there too? What had gotten into her?

She slowly looked up at the sky, her gaze drawn by the moon's light flooding through the cotton-woods. *The moon has gotten into you, Lila,* she told herself. The cold wind sent a shudder through her body. *Only the harvest moon.*

The reasoning sounded weak in her own mind, like an excuse, and her one consolation was that she'd never have to see the man again. The thought that she *might* see him again was too embarrassing to contemplate. Mortifying, actually, and ridden with guilt. No one had kissed her like that since Danny, and she wasn't ready to replace a widow's memories. Not again, never again.

One

A deep winter snow blanketed every square inch of the prairie, the gently rolling hills, and all the roads tying them together. Lila moved from room to room in the quiet dawn of Christmas Eve, starting the coffeemaker, turning up the heat, taking a moment to gaze at the white peaks of the Rockies standing like earthbound clouds against the sky.

She had a dozen presents still to wrap, and though she'd set her Christmas tree up in her new office, she decided to finish the chore in the much warmer kitchen. For reasons she couldn't explain, her office seemed to have a crosswind. She'd been meaning to call Dale Smith about it for weeks, but what with final exams and advising her master's students and doctoral candidates, the month of December had slipped by without a minute to spare. She had a feeling January was going to go the same way, at least she hoped so. Moping around the house had been an obsession the first year after Danny's death. It was not a habit she cared to fall into again, for last winter the antidote had proven to be more painful than the loneliness.

Christmas break was the worst, but she had a plan this year: work, work, and more work in her new office. She wasn't going to relax for a moment. Vigilance would keep her from doing anything stupid; she was sure of it. She was counting on it. Hadn't work kept her from dwelling—too much—on Jack Hudson and the magical kiss they'd shared one September evening? Hadn't work kept her from wondering if maybe he'd drop by, just to see how the office looked; and kept her from feeling disappointed when he didn't? Yes, it had. Work was the answer.

After she had all the presents rounded up on the kitchen table, she walked over to the counter to pour a cup of coffee. That was when she heard it, a low, grumbling noise, more a quiver in the air than a sound. She turned toward the doorway to her office, then stared in dumbstruck horror as her brand-new ten-by-twenty-foot addition peeled off the side of her house. The roof went first, dropping straight down and dumping a ton of snow onto her desk. The walls followed quickly, one at a time, buckling and groaning and collapsing inward in slow motion.

When it was all over and destruction lay across the land like the last invasion of Genghis Khan, she turned, silent and ashen-faced, to the telephone. Fingers stiff with anger, she punched in the seven numbers printed on the business card tacked to her kitchen bulletin board.

"This number is no longer in service. If you need—"

She slammed the phone down and whipped it back up, punching in the next seven numbers on the card with a vengeance, angrier than before, if that were possible.

How dare that damn carpenter change his phone number when every whipstitch of work she'd paid him for had just self-destructed! she railed silently. Well, somebody was going to hear about it, and if it wasn't that damn Dale Smith, it would be that damn Jack Hudson!

Five rings later, a muffled, tired voice answered. "Yeah?"

"Mr. Hudson?" She clipped off the name.

"Yeah?"

"Th-this—" Her voice broke. She paused to inhale a trembling breath before trying again, and the words verily hissed from between her tightly clenched jaws. "This is Dr. Singer. If you've got a lawyer, you'd better call him, and if you don't, you'd better get one, because I'm—I'm going to sue you and your partner *for every damn dime you've got.*"

"Who?"

"Dale Smith," she snapped, wondering what kind of idiot would forget his own partner's name. The wind picked up and blew across the demolished office and into the kitchen, making her colder and angrier.

"Smitty? Is that you?" Jack slowly rolled to a sitting position on the bed, holding his head with his free hand. He'd worked too late to be able to think at the crack of dawn. "You sound funny."

"N-no, Mr. Hudson," Lila said, hating the way

her voice was beginning to shake. She wrapped her arm tight around her waist. "This is Dr. Singer. Doc-tor Sing-er," she repeated a little louder, a little clearer.

The barest gleam of a light bulb clicked on in Jack's muddled brain. "Lila Singer?"

"Yes!" She got the word out between chattering teeth and huddled her backside up against the wall, hunching her shoulders down. She couldn't believe it. She couldn't believe anything as outrageously stupid as half her house falling off had happened to her. "I . . . I . . ." Her voice broke again, and she gave up in disgust.

Jack grinned and rubbed a hand over his eyes. He couldn't believe it. He couldn't believe the woman he'd kissed for no sane reason and hadn't been able to forget was calling him. Her timing was incredible, beating him to the punch by mere hours. He'd promised himself the luxury of calling her during the holidays, after his workload had eased up a bit.

He'd gone out to her place a couple of times in early October, supposedly to help Smitty. Each time Lila Singer hadn't been home, though, and each time he hadn't stayed longer than five minutes. Smitty hadn't seemed to want his help, and he'd felt foolish hanging around waiting for her. He was too old, he'd told himself, for crazy infatuations.

But he hadn't forgotten what it was like to kiss Lila Singer. The warmth, and taste, and welcoming softness of her mouth beneath his had felt too good, too right.

"Hi, Lila," he drawled, his voice still husky with sleep. "It's good to hear from you." And it was very good. "Quite a storm we've been having. Looks like a white Christmas this year."

Good to hear from her? Lila repeated silently. She tightened her mouth and shivered inside her flannel robe. He wasn't listening to her again. Refraining from the rare but succinct cussing on the tip of her tongue, she started to set him straight. "Mr. Hudson—"

"Jack, please," Jack interrupted with a yawn, all the while fighting an overactive imagination stimulated by her voice. It was damn early, barely six o'clock. She could be wearing anything.

Black lace would be perfect, he thought, with her dark hair and her soft, creamy skin . . . and that mouth. He shifted on the bed, then decided just to get up and head for the shower. Imagining Lila Singer in black lace had a way of taking the chill off the morning in a hurry.

"*Mr. Hudson*," she said clearly, "I am instigating legal action against you, and if you are not here in fifteen minutes, I'm going to call the police and have you arrested!"

The phone banged in Jack's ear. He winced and jerked the receiver away from his head. Arrested? He'd missed something. What had happened to the weather and black lace? He gave his head a slight shake. No, they hadn't been talking about black lace. He'd been imagining that part. But the weather had been real. A white Christmas, more snow than they'd had in twenty years, a heavy, wet snow, the kind that broke tree limbs and tested roofs, the kind that . . .

He did a mental backtrack and swore softly under his breath. Moving quicker than his brain told him was wise, he reached for his pants and shirt, praying the snowplows had worked all night. She'd given him only fifteen minutes before she'd call the cops.

Jack stood outside in the snow; then, without needing to open a door, walked inside to stand in more snow. Disaster was the only word that came to mind. Actually, a couple of other words did come to mind, words like liability, expensive, and damn Smitty. What had he been doing out there for the last three months? And where had all of Lila Singer's money gone? Certainly not into quality construction. He'd never seen a mess like the one tumbled all over her backyard and through her office.

"Three thousand dollars," she muttered, struggling past him with a computer console in her arms. Her full mouth didn't look the least bit kissable this morning. In fact, the lady looked like a small pot ready to boil over. Her movements were jerky, her muscles tight with anger.

Jack nodded in agreement, jotted the figure down on his small notepad, and wished he'd taken the time to fix himself a thermos of coffee. It was going to be a long day, and he didn't have the guts to ask Dr. Singer for a cup. Neither did he have the nerve to offer his help again, as he had when he'd first arrived. She'd made it clear what his job was, and it didn't include rescuing her office equipment or any of the hundreds of books scattered in the rubble.

Dr. Singer. He shook his head and continued looking around. More money than brains, and damn little money, had been his erroneous initial summation of her. The lady obviously had plenty of brains.

"Oh, no." The whispered wail came from behind him. He turned and found her kneeling by a pile of books. She lifted one and gently brushed the snow off its blue cover, revealing a gold-leaf border. "Oh, no," she repeated softly to herself, the first bit of softness she'd shown all morning.

"What's wrong?" he asked, and immediately felt stupid. What was wrong was all around him, some of it broken, most of it wet.

She flashed him an icy glance, the tightness returning to her mouth. "Edgar Rice Burroughs, *Son of Tarzan*, first edition, *formerly* in immaculate condition." She rose and wrapped her arms around the book. "Four hundred and fifty dollars."

Jack watched her stomp through the mess and into the house. "Four hundred and fifty dollars," he whispered, adding the number to the growing column on his notepad. He looked at the half ton of other books and prayed there weren't too many more four-hundred-fifty-dollar versions in the wreckage. He'd never heard of such a thing. Four hundred and fifty dollars for a book, and a Tarzan book at that. He'd seen the movies as a kid and thought they were pretty good, but not four hundred dollars worth of good. Maybe the books were better than the movies. He'd heard similar opinions about other movies from friends of his who read a lot.

He spent the next half hour combing through the broken lumber and found nothing to decrease his anger at Smitty. His partner, his best friend, had short-shrifted every aspect of the job. He'd bought third grade lumber and pieced it together into the worst excuse for a framing job Jack had ever seen. There was barely enough wood in the roof to hold up the shingles. There certainly hadn't been enough to hold up the Colorado snows. The whole damn room had crumbled under the weight.

Hudson and Smith Construction would no doubt crumble under it too. The mess piled around his feet was the result of negligence and fraud. Dr. Singer had paid good money for good construction, and even an unskilled eye could tell that the money had gone someplace else, probably into Smitty's pocket. They were doomed.

A sudden thought had him swearing. *They* weren't doomed. He was doomed all by himself. Smitty had said he needed to get away for a while, and he'd refused to say where he was going or how long he'd be gone. Jack was afraid the answer to the last question was a very long time. Divorce did crazy things to some people, crazy, criminal things.

Even in his anger, though, he felt pity for his friend. Running away never solved anything, and running away with somebody else's money only made the problem worse.

Well, he certainly wasn't going to have Smitty tracked down and arrested. Somehow he'd have to make good on the job. He looked at the destruction with a new eye and decided some of the materials were salvageable. With his insurance, a little cash out of his own pocket, and by pulling in some favors, he should be able to fulfill Lila Singer's wildest dreams of space. All he had to do was talk the lady into giving him a chance.

He turned toward the kitchen, but got no farther than three steps. The quiet, muffled sounds coming from somewhere in the house were horrifying and unmistakable. She was crying.

Sighing, he cast his eyes toward the blue Colorado sky peeking through the few remaining beams. Now what? he wondered, feeling helplessly in over his head. Tears had never been his forte, and Lila Singer's tears seemed to be affecting him more than most.

You never should have kissed her, Jack, he told himself, no matter how big the moon was last September. Now, three months later, he felt incredibly foolish. Why hadn't Smitty told him she was a professor at the university? And an English professor at that.

She certainly hadn't wasted any time in rattling off her credentials and her connections, when he arrived, all of them first class. She'd taken the high road with him the minute he'd stepped out of his truck. He didn't blame her. Given the same circumstances, he would have done the same thing. He didn't have any first-class credentials, though, and the only even remotely intimidating connection he had was his brother-in-law the policeman, whom she thankfully hadn't called.

And she was crying.

Jack lowered his chin to his chest and allowed himself another deep sigh. He felt like hell. He didn't want to face her tears and her four-hundred-fifty-dollar Tarzan book. He didn't want to face her Ph.D., and most of all he didn't want to face her big brown eyes and try to fast-talk her into giving him a chance.

But business was business, and a guy had to eat and keep a roof over his head. His glance strayed back up to the sky. Which was more than Hudson and Smith had done for Lila Singer.

Lila heard Jack Hudson call her name, and she hastily wiped the tears from her cheeks. Damn the man, did he have to invade the privacy of her sitting room? She'd made it clear where his place was, out there in the destruction of her office, not in here, where her heart was breaking every time she looked at Danny's book. A wave of guilt rolled over her sadness, sharpening both feelings. Another tear ran down her face.

She'd been so angry, and so concerned about her damned computer, she hadn't remembered his prized first edition until she'd stumbled over it. She'd wanted to forget the pain of Danny's death, but not him, not the things he'd held dear.

Her fingers trailed over the blue cover. Damp stains marred the cloth and loosened pieces of the gilt edging, ruining the perfection that once had been. If she'd only remembered sooner, before she'd wasted her time threatening Jack Hudson and crying on the phone to her mother, she might have saved the book.

She was going to forget that damn kiss and sue his pants off. She was going to take his business, his home, his truck, his—

"Dr. Singer?"

She stiffened at the sound of his voice behind her.

"What?" She laid the book on a small, ornately carved table and wiped her cheeks again, discreetly using an edge of her cuff and keeping her back to him. Her position on the floor in front of a matched pair of antique chairs helped to hide the action.

"I've looked the office over," he said, "and it's not as bad as it seemed at first. You didn't have your floor covering down yet, so that's going to save a lot. I've got a line on some bigger windows than the ones you lost, more like what you had in mind in the beginning." That's right, Jack, keep talking, he told himself. He ran his pencil down his list of figures and notes, trying to ignore how vulnerable she looked sitting on the rug with her legs beneath her. "I can have the walls and the roof back up by New Year's Eve, personally guaranteed work done by me. I'll call my window supplier today. I don't think he'll want to see me on Christmas, but I'll drive down to Denver the day after. My liability insurance should cover any personal item losses, and if it doesn't, I will."

As he talked, Lila slowly turned her head to look over her shoulder at him. It seemed the least amount of consideration she needed to expend on a man she was going to ruin. Sniffling, she gazed disdainfully at him.

"If you'd rather sue me than let me try to make it right," he continued, "I'll understand, no hard feelings. But I'd really like the chance to fix this, to build you the room we talked about last fall, to put some space into your house and the Rockies right in your lap."

He'd remembered, Lila thought, her disdain slipping a little. He'd remembered about the mountains. She shifted to one side and gave him more of her attention, maybe too much more. There was something innately masculine about him, standing there in his work boots and faded jeans, wearing an unpressed white shirt and a rumpled tie obviously meant to impress her. She wasn't accustomed to having strange men in her house, and his presence made her feel awkward in a way she hadn't felt in years. He'd had no business kissing her last fall—no matter how wondrous that kiss remained in her memory. It had gotten their relationship off to a bad start, especially since she was now being forced to sue him.

"I've got a few ideas you won't find in any store-bought plans," he went on, "and I'll give them to you at cost of materials, free labor, no bull." His boots were wet, she noticed, but he was careful not to stand on her imported Turkish rug. That was hardly the consummate sign of gentility, but it was a point in his favor. "By Valentine's Day," he said, "I can have you sitting in two hundred square feet of the office of your dreams."

"You've already had that chance," she informed him, working a trace of coolness into her tone.

Jack felt the ice and warmed to the challenge. "I know up to this point Hudson and Smith have been about the worst thing to happen to you, but it's just Hudson Construction now, and I can guarantee you won't find a better man to clean up the mess and get those walls back where they belong, and in record time. You don't owe me anything, but I owe you, and if we've got our assets all tied up in a lawsuit, it's going to be pretty tough for either one of us to get what we want."

There were a few too many "we's" flying around the room to suit Lila. "You're the one with the problem, Mr. Hudson."

"I know that. Jack."

"What?" She shot him a quizzical look.

"Jack. My name is Jack."

"I know your name, Mr. Hudson," she said,

dropping her gaze and absently smoothing her gray tweed slacks. She hoped she wouldn't have to get any ruder to make her point. He was starting to unnerve her. She should have called her lawyer and let him deal with Jack Hudson.

When he didn't respond, she hazarded another quick glance at him. He didn't seem the least bit disturbed by her discourtesy. In fact, she didn't think he'd heard her little riposte. He stood quiet and still, his gaze riveted to a place somewhere beyond and above her head. Even before she turned, she knew exactly what had captured his attention.

It wasn't black lace at all, Jack thought, staring at the life-size photograph hanging between two high windows. It was white gauze, streamers of it, as sheer and light as threads could be and still hold together as cloth. They swirled around her body, caressing ivory satin skin, barely covering the peaks of her breasts, catching on the lowest curve of her hip, exposing a midriff a man could believe in.

Jack believed. He'd been on the verge of conversion months before under a harvest moon, and the photograph of her looking more like his fantasies than even his own imagination could conjure up brought him completely into the fold.

Silver glitter graced her shoulders. Her riotous tumble of ebony curls was windblown and dappled with moonbeams. She was poised on tiptoe in profile, bending slightly forward at the waist, holding a wand of rainbow light to chase away the night mists and bestow her favors.

She was magic. The photographer had known it; the photographer had known her intimately. Jack had no doubts of that. Anyone might have captured the texture of her skin. Anyone might have dreamed up the lighting effects that made her shine in the mysterious darkness of the woodland setting. No one but a lover, though, brought such a look to a woman's face. He felt like a voyeur, and still he couldn't look away.

A flood of embarrassment pooled in Lila's cheeks and spread across her face. Thousands of people had seen Danny's photograph of her—it had been on exhibit in New York just last year in a retrospective of his work—but she didn't recall anyone taking such a *sensual* interest in it. Or maybe she was misinterpreting the intensity she saw in Jack Hudson's clear hazel eyes. Or maybe she wasn't. She wasn't sure, except of the intensity itself.

"Yes, well . . . Jack," she said, pushing herself off the floor. "I'm sure we'll be able to work something out." The strangeness of the words brought her up short. Damn, she thought. He had her on the run, on the defensive when all the facts were stacked in her favor.

Jack had seen enough. He was some kind of fool all right. He'd fantasized about Lila Singer for three months, and all the while she'd been with some guy who could make her look like that. It was starting out to be a real lousy Christmas. If her Ph.D. and the construction fiasco hadn't convinced him to forget his romantic intentions, the look on her face in the photograph came damn close. But some dreams died hard.

Lila stopped herself from retracting her words, a subtle change in Jack's gaze giving her pause. Defeat lingered there, a thoughtful defeat, a carefully weighed and accepted defeat, and despite her anger at him, she was surprised. Nothing in their encounters had led her to believe he was a man who knew much about defeat. On the contrary, he'd come across as one of the most arrogant, confident men she'd ever met.

She knew the smart move was to get rid of him, yet she hesitated.

Jack knew he might as well leave, yet he didn't.

"I—"

"I—"

They both spoke at once, but Jack was the first to grin. What the hell? he thought. He couldn't lose what he'd never had.

"I'd like you to give me a chance," he said. "One week. If you don't like the work at that point, you're welcome to sue me."

There was absolutely no moon showing in the morning sky, nothing to blame it on except a budding curiosity Lila found impossible to deny.

"You've got a deal." She stuck out her hand and was rewarded with his strong, warm grip.

She'd survived some of the worst life had to offer. She'd certainly survive a few hours and days here and there of Jack Hudson's company, as long as he kept his distance. And as long as she kept hers.

The unexpected thought startled her, and she quickly dropped his hand. Say what she might, she hadn't forgotten what it had felt like to be kissed by him. She hadn't forgotten how she'd clung to him, or the taste of him on her lips.

"You'll—you'll have to excuse me, Mr. Hudson," she stammered, backing away from him. "I need to get over to my parents'. I'd appreciate it if you could fix the hole in my house before you leave."

Jack nodded, wishing she hadn't released his

hand and wondering what the color staining her cheeks meant. Maybe he was wrong about the photographer. Even the possibility was enough to lift his spirits. One thing was certain, though. He'd just bought himself enough time to find out.

Two

New Year's Eve, Lila thought with a pained sigh. She pulled up next to the Hudson Construction truck and braked to a slow halt. Who would have thought he'd work on New Year's Eve? Didn't everyone else in the world besides her have something big planned for New Year's Eve?

She should be used to him by now, but she wasn't. Not even close. An all too familiar queasiness invaded her stomach.

She'd bowed out early on her parents' yearly countdown and had planned on a quiet evening at home, reminiscing, reading Blake or Shakespeare, maybe allowing a few tears in her wine. She had hoped on this one day to avoid the curious awareness Jack Hudson's presence had aroused in her all week.

It wasn't to be. True to his word, he hadn't let up, even on the holidays. In one week he'd given her more office than Dale Smith had in three months. She had more windows, bigger windows, compliments of Hudson Construction. Something that looked suspiciously like a skylight was taking shape in her roof, compliments of Hudson Construction. A delicate French door had taken the place of her cheap glass and metal sliding abomination, compliments of Hudson Construction. All the work was beautifully conceived and executed, a cut above anything else she'd seen. The man was an artist with a two-by-four and a handful of nails. She'd known an hour after he'd started that she wasn't going to sue him. She just hoped she didn't bankrupt him.

She stepped out of her Jeep and felt a bevy of snowflakes blow up under her wool skirt and melt on her knees. She'd ask him to leave, that was all. She'd just ask him to leave. It was her house, even if he had practically been living there since Christmas.

She closed the driver's door and stood for a moment in the falling snow, watching him through the windows. He *had* practically moved in on her. He was there first thing in the morning, offering doughnuts she always declined. He'd taken to keeping a six-pack of beer in her refrigerator, after he'd asked and she hadn't had the nerve to tell him no. Twice he'd asked to use her microwave to heat his supper. And he'd worked nonstop, hammer falling in cadence, tape measure snapping, saw buzzing through lumber.

Tonight, though, there was absolutely no reason that she should have to put up with him hanging around her house and doing all those things he did all day, like interrupting her work to ask her opinion, or making her feel guilty by shoveling the walk on his way out. He wasn't doing penance, for crying out loud. He was trying to keep her from ruining him.

She would simply ask him to leave.

Jack poured the last of his coffee out of the thermos and looked around the office. He'd done a helluva job, if he said so himself. Walls stood where recently there had been only rubble and air.

He sipped his coffee, letting the fragrant steam warm his nose and cheeks. He'd known the instant Lila had come home, and he was trying hard not to count the minutes until she entered the house, a habit he'd fallen into. It was doubly hard this night, because he hadn't expected her to come home at all. It was New Year's Eve, and he couldn't imagine even the world's busiest photographer leaving his lady alone on the biggest date night of the year. His own dateless status was a lot easier to explain. The only woman he'd wanted to ask out for months was Lila Singer. Walls surrounding her office would have been a definite step in the right direction, if he hadn't had the photographer to worry about too.

The door opened behind him, and he slowly turned.

The first thing Lila noticed was the music. It was always the same, oldies rock and roll, and more than once she'd caught him tapping his feet or swinging his hips with the beat. She preferred her music with a little more age on it, about two or three hundred years' worth, and she couldn't remember the last time she'd swung her hips to anything other than an aerobics routine.

The second thing she noticed was the temperature in the office. The place was almost warm again. The third and most striking thing she noticed was his smile. He never failed to smile, and she never failed to notice it. Never failed to notice his mouth. Never failed to remember that kiss . . . The queasiness in her stomach increased. The man was going to drive her right over the edge.

"Hi."

"Hi," she answered. "I . . . uh, didn't expect you to be working tonight."

"No date." He shrugged and blessed her with another easy smile. "How about you?"

The man was too direct for polite company, but Lila managed to hold her own. "I don't date."

If she'd said "I don't rape and plunder," Jack might have understood the frostiness of her tone, but she'd said "date" and made it sound like the sin of the century. He was confused . . . and intrigued.

"Engaged?" he asked, and took another sip of coffee.

"I beg your pardon?" she replied, and it was the only reply she intended to give. With the right inflection that phrase could effectively shut down any conversation.

"Engaged," he repeated. "As in fiancé."

She'd obviously missed her inflection. "No. I am not engaged."

How anyone could look so cuddly and be so damned prickly was beyond him, Jack thought. "So, you're not engaged and you don't date." He broadened his grin. "What do you do on Friday nights, and Saturdays, and New Year's Eve?" What he didn't ask, though it was at the top of his list, was—*Who is the photographer and what does he do to make you look like that?* If the truth be known, when she wasn't home he'd stood in her sitting room more than once and stared at the photograph.

Lila let out a small sigh. She had not only failed to kick Jack out or at least shut down the conversation, but in less than a minute he had directed said conversation beyond her range of approved topics. She should never have allowed him to kiss her. It made him think he could take all sorts of liberties.

"I work, Mr. Hudson," she said, drawing herself up to her full height, "which is what I need to do now, without the distraction of *your* work. So if you don't mind, I'd like you to stop for the evening." Two, she decided, could play at being direct.

"Fine with me," he said, still grinning, "but what are you going to do about him?" He lifted his coffee cup and gestured toward the driveway.

Lila turned her head, and an unintentional groan escaped her lips. She'd thought Jack Hudson was the last person on earth she'd want to see tonight. She'd been wrong.

Trey Farris, her very own personal, overardent teaching assistant, stumbled twice in the snow while trying to find the makeshift porch of concrete blocks leading to the French doors. He waved after each stumble, and Lila lifted her hand in return, plastering a false smile on her face. She had hoped to have the four weeks of Christmas break as a vacation from fending off Trey's not very subtle advances. Jack Hudson may have outmaneuvered her for a few minutes, but she couldn't let Trey have even an inch of leeway. The graduate student had the camping instincts of an Eagle Scout. Once he settled in, she'd never get rid of him, and if he breathed on her neck one more time, she'd probably hit him. She had about thirty seconds to think of an excuse to get rid of him.

"Do whatever you have to. I'll back you up." Jack's voice came from behind her, and she gave him a startled glance over her shoulder.

No, she thought, looking into those hazel eyes shot through with flecks of green and gold. She'd be crazy to make any kind of illicit pact with him, or to engage in anything as intimate as a lie. One kiss had been more than enough of that kind of business.

Jack saw a slight tension tighten her mouth and the barest hint of desperation darken her eyes. He'd caught her between a rock and a hard place, between himself and the gangly young man flailing his way through the snow. By her reaction, Jack surmised the teaching assistant obviously was not the photographer, and Jack was powerfully curious to know which path Lila Singer would find the least dangerous.

He was still willing to bet money she and the photographer had something going, but she'd just admitted to not being engaged, and he knew she wasn't married. He would have noticed a husband, or at least signs of a husband. The lady lived alone . . . and she looked great in peach-colored sweaters with pearly sequins. Really great.

The sequins swirled down one shoulder and across the front of the sweater. The matching peach-colored skirt was tight, his favorite style. Gray suede high-heeled boots gave her a few more inches, and her full-length mink coat looked like just the sort of thing he'd love to wrap his arms around, especially with her in the middle of it. All in all, he was probably outclassed, and his imagination was definitely out of line.

And she was out of time.

At the sound of a knock, they both shifted their attention to the door and the young man letting himself inside.

"Hi, Dr. Singer." He stamped his tennis shoes on the bare plywood floor, leaving behind big clumps of snow. "I was in the neighborhood and thought I'd better come by and see how you were doing. I hated to think of you snowed in all by yourself, especially on New Year's Eve."

"How thoughtful," she replied in her usually cool tone, and Jack had to give the kid a couple of points for sheer guts or sheer idiocy. The young man must have known what he was getting into with Miss Prickly Puss, and he'd still dragged himself through the biggest snowstorm of the century to get out there and be shot down. He must want her very badly. Jack didn't blame him for that. The more he saw of Lila Singer, the more he thought about wanting her too. As a matter of fact, that was exactly what he was thinking about even as the kid was making his big play.

"I brought some wine," he said, pulling a bottle out of his voluminous, heavy wool coat. "A gift, actually. I came by Christmas Day, but you weren't here. Glad to see your house is getting back together."

Jack refrained from a snort of laughter. The kid was about as smooth as corn whiskey. Jack hadn't used the old "don't call first or she'll make an excuse" ploy since high school, and "gangly legs" had just admitted to using it twice. The wine, though, didn't bring laughter to mind. He raised one eyebrow as he saw the two-digit price tag, then gave the kid a more thorough assessment, wondering if there was more competition in the room than he'd thought.

"Thank you, Trey," Lila said, accepting the wine bottle, "but we were just getting ready to—"

"Oh, wow," Trey whispered, touching his fingers to his head and bringing them away smeared with blood. Jack had to give him two more points for originality, but he could have killed the kid for interrupting her. She'd said "we," and he was the only available "we" around, and he sure would have loved to hear what they had been just about ready to do. On the other hand, he was a little disturbed that she thought he'd be easier to handle than the novice he was up against.

"For goodness' sakes," she exclaimed, using the soft, soft tone he heard all too rarely. "Come inside where it's warm. What happened? Did you do that on the steps?" She tucked her arm through Trey's and led him into the main part of the house, leaving Jack standing alone in the roughed-out addition. But not for long.

He finished his coffee with one swallow and set the cup on a stack of lumber. Then, without hesitation, he followed the wounded dove and Florence Nightingale inside, flipping off the switch to the single bulb hanging in the office. The kid may be up on him about four to zip, but he hadn't won the war. And Jack's masculine instincts told him this was war, the real simple two men, one woman, and one night kind of war.

"Lila went to get some first aid supplies," Trey said to Jack when he entered the kitchen. Trey looked smug and as happy as a tick on a dog, despite the thin trickle of blood coursing down his brow. "You must be the guy fixing her office."

"Yeah." Jack gave him a big smile and a good, firm handshake. "Jack Hudson. And you are?"

"Trey Farris. Lila's teaching assistant. We work together at the university." He opened a cupboard door and lifted down two wineglasses. "She's helping me with my master's thesis. We get together quite a bit to toss around ideas and things. I don't suppose you know much about nineteenth-century British literature."

"Not much," Jack agreed, not fooled by the younger man's line of bull. He'd caught the formal greeting of "Dr. Singer" at the door. The only thing Trey Farris had sewn up with Lila Singer was a job. Which was about the same thing Jack had sewn up with her.

"Everybody at the university heard about the screwup on the construction," Trey continued, working the cork out of the wine bottle. He stopped every twist or two to push up the sleeves on his fuzzy gray sweater. Everything he wore bagged and sagged, and he seemed incapable of keeping his glasses on his nose. "Lila was pretty upset. We all thought she should get somebody else to . . ."

Trey droned on and on, but Jack quit listening. He was too busy wondering if he should pop the kid, or just grab him by the collar and scare him enough to make him rethink his conversation. The kid had nerve, too much nerve, and he was beginning to irritate the hell out of Jack, especially with the two wineglasses bit.

Lila came back in the nick of time, saving Jack

from some macho foolishness and Trey from getting his intellectual attitude mussed up.

"Have a seat over here, Trey," she said, "by the breakfast counter. I'm so sorry about those steps. Mr. Hudson?" She turned to Jack, and he knew he winced. Mr. Hudson, Mr. Hudson. It was going to drive him crazy. "Maybe you should build a handrail to keep any more accidents from happening."

Jack stopped himself from saying something about lovestruck young studs forgetting where their feet were and said only, "Good idea."

Trey smirked behind Lila's back and began pouring wine into the two glasses he'd taken with him to the breakfast counter. Jack did his best to level him with a dark glare.

For her part, Lila concentrated on her ministrations. She possibly dabbed at Trey's forehead with more force than was necessary, but she was upset. She wasn't blind or comatose. She felt the undercurrents running between the two men, and she found them incomprehensible, disconcerting, and somewhat scandalous. No one had a claim on her. What were they thinking?

On second thought, she didn't want to know.

"I don't think that's a good idea, Trey," she said when he picked up one of the wineglasses. "You have a nasty bump on your head, and the roads are treacherous."

"Nasty bump," Jack repeated with another big smile, leaning over to relieve the younger man of his wineglass. "Treacherous roads." He settled his hips back against the counter and sipped the wine.

"I'll be back in a minute," Lila said. "I forgot the

antiseptic." She swept out of the kitchen, ignoring both of them as best she could.

Trey didn't waste a moment staking his claim. "I've known Lila for a long time . . . a very long time," he said meaningfully, pressing forward on the counter. "And I don't think she's ready for some guy like you to push his way into her life."

"What kind of guy is that?" Jack wasn't offended by the kid's bluntness. As a matter of fact, he gave him a few more points for audacity and astute intuition.

"Well," Trey started slowly, as if measuring his words and the distance between himself and Jack. "You're a carpenter, right?"

"Right." Jack was beginning to get offended.

"Well, Lila isn't exactly the carpenter type. I mean, Danny Singer wasn't what you'd call an average joe. The man had shows in New York, Los Angeles, Chicago. The photographs he took of Lila sported price tags of twenty-five hundred dollars, and that was *before* he died. The stuff is probably priceless now, and . . . Well, that's the kind of man Lila is used to. Cultured, intellectual, academic even. Have you caught my drift?"

Jack was busy absorbing the ton of information he'd just received, about rich photographers who were dead and Lila Singer being a widow, but he'd caught the kid's drift loud and clear. "I think so," he said carefully, then paused for a swallow of wine. "Correct me if I'm wrong, but what we've got here is a kid who can't even dress himself right hiding behind a hundred years of overseas fiction and trying his damnedest 'to make' the teacher along the way, a kid who can't even find four feet of concrete porch without falling on his swollen head, and somehow this jerk thinks he's got something over a guy who works for a living. Does that about sum it up?"

Lila's return stole Trey's chance to answer, which was probably just as well. The lady's timing was proving to be the only thing keeping the evening at all polite and civil.

"This may sting a little, but it's all I have." She poured the antiseptic on a cotton ball and squashed it onto Trey's forehead. "I'm very sorry this happened, but if you'll go straight home and take a couple of aspirin, you'll probably feel fine in the morning."

"I feel fine now, Dr. Singer, really. It's just a scrape."

"I don't think we should take a chance," Lila insisted. "Especially with me being the liable party."

"Oh, you don't have to be the liable party," Trey said, and gestured at Jack. "I'll sue him."

That did it.

Jack pushed away from the counter and picked the kid's coat up off a chair. "I'll help you out to your car."

"But I'm not—"

"Oh, thank you, Mr. Hudson," Lila interrupted. "I don't think he should try those steps on his own again, not without a handrail."

Jack nodded and hustled Trey out of his chair and into his coat. What resistance he felt in the bony little body, he overcame with a bit of subtle strong-arming.

"But, Dr. Sing—"

Jack quickly nudged the back of Trey's knee with his own knee, effectively disabling Trey for a couple of seconds so he could snag the kid's arms in the sleeves of his big coat.

"Goodness!" Lila lunged for Trey and caught him at the same time that Jack pulled his coat over his shoulders. "Why, you can barely stand up. Are you sure you can drive?"

"I'm fine, I swear," Trey gritted through his teeth, giving Jack a black look and shaking the bigger man's hands off with a quick jerk of his shoulders. Then he reconsidered his statement. "Well, maybe I am a little wooz—"

"You're fine," Jack interrupted, giving him a good clap on the back. "I can tell. You young kids are made of stern stuff. A couple of aspirin and you'll be great. Come on. I'll get you across the porch without breaking any bones."

"I bet," Trey muttered.

"Thank you, Jack."

Jack. Finally, he thought, Jack. Her use of his first name put a measure of determination in his step, and he had Trey out the door, down the stairs, across the backyard, and into his car before the kid had a chance to regroup.

"Nice meeting you, Trey," he said. "Don't forget to take those aspirin."

"Wait a minute, buddy." The kid speedily rolled down his window and grabbed Jack by the sleeve. "That was a twelve-dollar bottle of wine."

Laughter checked Jack's anger in an instant. He shoved a hand into his jeans pocket and pulled out a ten and a five, chuckling under his breath. "You've got good taste, kid. Keep the tip." He loved being generous in victory. It was a hell of a lot better than being generous in defeat.

Trey took the money and shoved it into his coat

pocket. "Yeah, well, just remember what I said, man. You're no Danny Singer."

It was a cheap shot, the cheapest; a low blow, the lowest; and it hit home with unerring accuracy. Jack didn't care much for the kid's presumptuous, intellectual categorizing, and he didn't know anything about dealing with widows. But he did know he'd never come close to what he'd seen in the magical photograph of Lila Singer dressed in ethereal gauze in the moonlight.

"Right, kid," he said, leaning over the open window. "Now, why don't you give this thing a little gas, and let's see if we can get you out of here before I change my mind about keeping you in one piece."

Lila stood on tiptoe at the kitchen counter, peeking out the window over the sink, not certain if she'd won or lost. Getting rid of Trey was a definite plus, but Jack Hudson was a definite unknown.

She took another sip of wine and tried to think of a polite way to thank him and kick him out at the same time. The man unnerved her in some very private places, places she'd forgotten about, and she didn't have a clue as to why. Sure, he was good-looking in an all-American way: broad and rugged in the shoulders, independent behind the eyes, and plain cute everywhere else. But that was no reason for her pulse to skip, or her breathing to quicken whenever she was around him. No reason at all.

She stretched higher on her tiptoes, craning her neck to one side to watch Jack give Trey's car an extra push out of the driveway. Her problem was she'd become too used to her students, graduate or otherwise. With them there was always an unspoken barrier, an undeniable difference in experience and authority. Jack Hudson didn't seem to recognize those things, even though she was the boss.

Or was she?

"Damn," she whispered. He was coming back into the house. She quickly swallowed the rest of her wine and set the glass aside. She'd thank him, that's what she'd do. There was absolutely no reason for him to hang around any longer. She'd just thank him and, of course, he'd take the hint and leave.

Of course he would, she assured herself, pausing to straighten the bottom of her sweater and smooth her skirt. As a matter of fact, he was probably coming in only to get his coat and his lunchbox.

The French doors opened with a squeak of newness. Drawing in a fortifying breath, Lila marched toward the office to thank him for all his trouble and his help. She got no farther than the connecting doorway, for there he was, standing next to a stack of lumber, picking up his lunchbox and putting on his battered black ski jacket. She didn't believe it. Neither did she believe the ache of disappointment she felt tightening her chest.

Jack heard a soft sound of dismay and looked up. Lila stood in the doorway, backlit by the glow from the kitchen, with the light tangled through her hair like a net of silver. In that instant she conjured up a thousand new feelings in his heart and body.

Hell, he thought. It's New Year's Eve.

He set his lunchbox back on the boards and walked over to her.

"I think the kid will be okay," he said.

"Me too," Lila whispered, though she hadn't meant to use such an intimate tone of voice. Whispering had a way of drawing another person near.

Jack obliged, ever so slightly. "Tomorrow is the last day I can work full-time over here," he said, resting his hand high on the doorjamb.

"Oh."

"I've got some other jobs I need to get back to."

"I *have* some other jobs," she softly corrected him.

He quirked one eyebrow in question. "At the university?"

"What?"

He grinned, slow and easy, and she felt a wave of heat spread across her face and chest. "Well, I guess it doesn't matter. I'll be over in the evenings to finish up."

"Okay." She'd lost the thread of the conversation somewhere, but it really didn't matter, not when he was standing so close in the half-dark room.

"I'll work on the handrail tomorrow."

He shifted his weight subtly, moving a couple of inches closer to her. She watched the smile fade from his face, and wondered if she could possibly be wanting what she thought she was wanting.

"If it's okay with you," he continued, "I'll keep my key to the French doors until the whole job is finished."

"That'll be fine." Her voice grew softer, her eyes

wider, and Jack found himself edging even closer, wishing he had a reason to touch her.

"I've been thinking of building in some bookcases," he murmured, absently lifting a hand to brush the wild curls back from her cheek. He needed no more reason than desire to touch her, he realized.

"Nice . . ." was all Lila managed to breathe out. His caress mesmerized her, like a magic spell.

He leaned down and brushed his mouth across her cheek. His hand tilted her chin up until their lips barely met. "You're too beautiful not to be kissed," he whispered, his voice husky with the same tension Lila felt with every breath. "Especially on New Year's Eve."

His hand slid to the nape of her neck as his mouth claimed hers in a series of teasing explorations. Lila found her reasoning powers melting with every light kiss he feathered across her lips. Each brief touch fanned a flame deep inside her, evoking once more the memories of a long-ago moonlit night when a stranger had kissed her and seemed not to be a stranger at all. His mouth rubbed against hers, warm and breathy, gentle and demanding. His tongue tasted her lips, and she sighed, granting him what he asked for.

In the way dusk slips into darkness, gentleness turned into passion and memories into a startling present. Lila felt the muscles in his arms flex as he gathered her closer. She felt her own heart beating a new rhythm, and she heard his breath grow ragged and heavy as he kissed her deeper, longer, slower. She reached for him to steady her world, but found the hardness of his body even further disorienting. It had been too long, and he felt too good. The size and strength of him was overpowering and protective at the same time. The circle of his arms was a homecoming, a haven to which she'd returned.

What was left of her rational mind insisted that this man was still a stranger, but coursing through the lost recesses of her soul was a remembrance of his slightest touch, of the way his mouth moved, the scent of him . . . Or was it an expectation, an instinctive knowledge of what was to come and the satisfaction of his fulfillment?

She didn't know, and truth be told, as he kept on kissing her, she didn't care.

Jack cared. He cared about her hair sliding through his fingers. He cared about her sweet curves pressed against him and driving him crazy. He cared about the wild abandon of her kiss and the way he was starting to lose control.

One more minute, he told himself, just one more minute of tasting her, of feeling the excitement she generated like heat under a summer sun. He slanted his mouth across hers in the opposite direction, and she followed him down the new path, molding her body to his in that one extra degree he couldn't handle. He'd never known a kiss to get out of hand so fast. He'd never known himself to get out of hand so fast.

"Lila . . ." He couldn't tear himself away.

"Jack?" she murmured, her mouth still touching his, and he knew she'd never forget his name again.

"Do you think—" He stopped, unsure of the right words, and kissed her again. When they came up for air, he knew he had to ask. "Lila, how do you feel about making love . . . with me, tonight? I mean . . ." Hell, he didn't know what he meant, so he kissed her again, and again, all the while trying to get it straight in his head about where his mind and his body were conflicting. Three more seconds of holding her in his arms proved his body thought his mind was nuts. His body had no doubts about wanting her, about how and where to touch her for the maximum effect, for a response guaranteed to leave tracks of fire across his senses. His body said, "Lift her skirt, Jack. Run your hand up her thigh and show her how good love can be with you."

His mind insisted on being a gentleman, of reminding him she was a widow and that she barely knew him, on giving her time, on promising the end would be worth the wait. Yet even as his mind took its noble stand, his hand slid down the side of her skirt.

Three

Lila gasped, not knowing if it was in shock or pleasure. His fingers grazed the curve of her hip, his palm rubbed slow, sensuous circles on the fabric of her skirt. Her body picked up the rhythm as he drew her deeper under the spell of his touch and his kiss.

Then, as if a transmission had finally made its delayed connection, his words penetrated the cloud of passion fogging her brain. She stiffened in his arms, though her mouth remained on his.

Jack felt the stilling of her lips and knew exactly what had happened. He opened his eyes the barest degree. Chocolate-brown eyes gazed back at him, wide with an emotion he couldn't name, until he noted the flush of embarrassment coursing across the delicate pale skin of her face. He closed his eyes and kissed her again, softly, telling her silently that he wanted her but was willing to let her go.

His insides remained on overdrive, and it took

him a moment longer to finally break contact. When he did he knew he had to do something besides stand and stare at her like a man who'd just seen water after twenty years in the desert. He'd probably frightened her, coming on like a randy teenager.

He had frightened her, but Lila knew it was a poor second to how badly she had scared herself by reacting to him as she had. Her breath was coming short and shallow, a dead giveaway to his effect on her. Yet even with the hot flush of humiliation staining her cheeks, she couldn't step away.

She looked up at him, watching him watch her, feeling like two people. One of those people had seldom gazed into his hazel eyes, barely knew his face, the straight nose, the gentle grin playing about a mouth that looked thoroughly kissed. Her blush heightened, but she didn't look away, for the other person knew him like the earth knows rain. It was that knowledge that frightened her. A sensual being inside her knew the pleasure of his thigh against hers, the light touch of his tongue on her lips, the heavier, drugging passion when his tongue invaded her mouth with primitive, consuming thrusts; a sensual being who had reacted instinctively to his every touch. And her instincts were the last thing Lila trusted. They'd been scorched and manhandled by grief. They'd led her into shame and degradation, and she planned on never taking the trip again.

Jack sensed her embarrassment turning to confusion and then pain, and he knew he needed to do something, and quickly. So he spoke in an attempt to give his mouth an alternative to touching hers again in a comforting caress. He spoke before he became completely lost in the soul-deep darkness of her eyes, before he'd actually given sufficient thought to his words.

"I could kiss you all night long."

His voice was husky and sincere enough to singe Lila's sensibilities with another wave of heat.

"It's . . . it's just a physical thing," she stammered, trying and failing to discount the emotions swamping her.

"Very physical," he agreed, his grin broadening.

"A purely chemical reaction," she continued.

"No, I flunked chemistry. I think this is something else."

"You flunked chemistry?"

"Among other things."

"Oh." Disappointment softened her voice, and Jack suddenly wished he'd done better in school, a thought that hadn't crossed his mind in fifteen years. Maybe if he'd known he'd someday fall for a college professor, he'd have tried harder, even though at the time it had seemed as if he were trying his hardest and getting damn little to show for it.

"I do have my good points," he said, only half teasing.

"I'm sure you do." She glanced away, but he wasn't ready to lose her for the night.

He brushed her cheek with his hand, urging her to meet his gaze. "I've been in business for ten years, and you're the first disaster I've had. I'm beginning to think it's the best thing to ever happen to me."

Her blush deepened, and she looked away again.

"I coach Little League," he added in a coaxing tone. "My mother loves me, and my ex-wife doesn't hate me." A true testimonial if he'd ever heard one, but its effect wasn't what he'd bargained for either.

Her head came up sharply. "You're divorced?"

Not the crime of the century in his book, but she made it sound like a federal offense. "Only once," he teased, but he could tell by the look on her face that he'd dug himself into a hole. He wasn't sure exactly why or how he'd gotten off on such a cockamamie subject with a woman he wanted to kiss again as soon as possible.

Lila shook her head. "I'd like you to leave." It was a lie, she admitted, but only half of one. Part of her did want him to leave, desperately, while the other half of her wanted just as desperately for him to kiss her once more.

"And I'd like to take you out tomorrow night," he said.

"I don't date." The statement sounded ridiculous now, even to her own ears, but she held by her credo.

"You don't date," he repeated after a long, tense pause, and she detected a note of anger in his voice. "But you'll kiss to the point of spontaneous combustion. I'm not complaining, mind you, but you might be *safer* dating, Dr. Singer."

Unwittingly, on a surge of adrenaline, she lifted her hand to slap him. Just as quickly, though, she curled her fingers and dropped her hand, abashed and confused.

"Okay," Jack said calmly, angry at himself for saying such a stupid thing.

"You don't understand." Her face was white, and she'd clenched her hands together so tightly, each knuckle stood out in stark relief.

"I'd like to understand." He reached for her, but she backed away.

"I'm sorry, really. I'd like you to leave."

"If you want to talk, I'm a good listener."

"No, thank you." She took another step backward, and Jack conceded defeat.

He turned and walked over to the stack of lumber where he'd left his lunchbox. Before he let himself out the French doors, though, he stopped and glanced over his shoulder. "You know, Lila," he said, a slight smile curving a corner of his mouth, "not even my mother got that upset about my flunking chemistry."

It was a second-rate attempt at humor, but Lila grabbed for it, partly out of appreciation for the attempt, partly out of contrition for the dreadful act of almost slapping him. He hadn't deserved to take the brunt of her anger, especially since it had been directed at herself more than at him.

"I'll get over it," she said with a weak smile of her own.

It was more than Jack had expected, but then, she was turning out to be more than he'd expected. Back in September he'd thought her all sweetness and serenity. Tonight she'd shown her fire, and he found himself drawn to the heat of her flames with an even greater force than he'd been drawn to the light of her sweetness.

Lila knew she had to forgive herself, but she wasn't sure how or where to begin. Time helped, and Jack gave her a week of it. Twice he left messages on her answering machine to explain his absence and to confirm his return on Friday.

Twice she listened to his rich, deep voice, the western drawl slow and easy, the timbre soothing like a river of honey. Twice she listened to him call her Lila, not Dr. Singer. She tried not to think about it. They obviously had nothing in common, which was her preferred standing for their relationship.

Nothing in common except those kisses.

The wayward thought intruded Friday evening as she stared out the sitting room window at the midnight-blue winter evening, her fingers tight around a heavy white envelope.

Piles of books and papers were spread out on the desk she'd moved back into the sitting room. Curriculum notes covered her end tables—British fiction on the one next to the fireplace, myth and Bible on the one between her brocade love seat and chair. Someday she hoped to teach Shakespeare, but she was in no position to make requests. In truth, she was grateful just to have her job. Even with her tenure, the university had been under enormous pressure last year to force her resignation.

She'd been such a blind, stupid fool. She, who'd always prided herself on her intelligence, had fallen for a handsome face and the oldest trick in the book.

With a small sound of disgust she turned away from the window, then whirled back around. It was Jack. Her heart started racing as she watched his truck round the corner into her driveway. Her gaze dropped to the envelope.

Coward, she accused herself, but there was nothing she could do. She didn't have the courage to face him, and for whatever reasons, she'd dawdled and revised the letter until it was far too late to mail it.

Before she could change her mind, she walked swiftly into the office and laid the letter on the stack of lumber where Jack always put his lunch-box. She'd written plainly and concisely. He couldn't fail to understand. She'd informed him that their contract, oral as it had been, was termi-nated. He'd done sufficient work to compensate her loss. She would hire the finish work out and still feel she'd gotten the best of the bargain. His building expertise had far surpassed her expecta-tions. He'd built her office as if it were meant to last a thousand years. Then she'd thanked him and signed off with "sincerely," and somewhere between the salutation and the closing she'd worked in a brief but heartfelt apology for almost slapping him. She hadn't mentioned their two "misunderstandings," and she certainly hadn't re-ferred to them as kisses.

Kisses . . . The word slipped across her mind like a silent whisper, and her fingers slowly curled into a fist. Lord, the man knew how to kiss . . . remarkably.

The sound of a slamming truck door jerked her out of her reverie, and Lila quickly disappeared back into the main part of the house.

If the lady won't go out on a date, bring the date to her, Jack thought, juggling a floppy pizza box, a six-pack of beer, a container of salad, and a smaller container of Rudi's Pizzeria's famous thick and creamy gorgonzola dressing. Being a connoisseur of pizza by necessity, he knew Rudi's was good.

The beer was imported and expensive. But the salad was the pièce de résistance: lettuce, tomatoes, cherry peppers, salami, pepperoni, provolone, big chunky croutons, black olives, and the gorgonzola dressing. No woman could resist Rudi's salad. It had the acceptable cachet of being a salad, but it was richer than sin.

Dessert was richer than double sin, a Kahlua truffle torte that was no torte at all, but a melt-in-your-mouth concoction of bittersweet chocolate and mystery. Irresistible.

He let himself into the office and walked across the cold plywood floor to set the pizza on the space heater. Then he carried the heater closer to the door leading to the rest of the house and knelt down to turn on the heat. If he'd had a fan, he would have used it to waft the tantalizing aroma in her direction. It was all part of his plan.

The lady did not want to be pushed. He'd had all week to figure out and digest that particular piece of information, so he'd decided to pull instead. He would be low key, easygoing, and available. Very available. He'd be there if she needed a friend or a shoulder to lean on. He wouldn't make any more passes that ended up with him becoming so aroused, he forgot to think and nearly got his face slapped. Yet she'd been so hot and sweet in his arms, even the memory of their kisses sparked a physical reaction in him.

He stood abruptly, ran a hand through his hair, and reminded himself that patience was a virtue. Pizza was the bait that night, not the incredible fireworks they made when their mouths and bodies rubbed up against each other.

Lord knew he was no saint, he'd never claimed

to be, but he'd always been discriminating when it came to women, love, and making love. His response to Lila Singer made him wonder if he'd lost the ability to distinguish between lust and longing, love and desire, wanting and needing, between the woman herself and what she did to him with each kiss.

He remembered loving and wanting Jessica Daniels in the eleventh grade until he'd thought his manhood and his heart would both break into a thousand pieces if he didn't have her. He'd been wrong. Jessica Daniels had never realized he was on the planet. He'd followed her into and flunked out of chemistry for nothing, and he'd remained intact for the next love down the line.

Marriage had been different in every way. He still missed a lot of things about marriage: having someone sharing his home, someone special, an ally through good times and bad—until things got really bad. And without admitting to being a chauvinist, he missed a woman's cooking. He missed it a lot. Women cooked differently from men. They put more love and less ego into it, and they actually followed recipes. It was a noticeable difference.

Lila Singer was a noticeable difference too. Being in love with her was out of the question. Love took longer than two kisses, three months of fantasies, and a week of unanswered phone calls. He was definitely fascinated, though, definitely intrigued, and he definitely wanted her. He felt possessive and protective. She touched him in places he hadn't expected and in ways he hadn't experienced, and with only her kiss. She'd shown magic for her husband. Without knowing what it was at the time, Jack had felt the remnants of that magic under a harvest moon, and he couldn't help but want, or need, to bring it back to full power.

He also needed to eat some pizza before the smell drove him crazy. He turned around to drop his gloves on the lumber he'd been using as a makeshift table, noticed the envelope, and his enthusiasm for the evening did a steady nosedive. Letters were not his favorite form of communication, especially when they came from someone he'd been looking forward to seeing all week.

He picked up the envelope and studied the letters looped and swirled across the front. It was his name all right, Jack and Hudson, which was barely a step above Mr. and Hudson. With a short sigh he shoved the envelope into his shirt pocket.

"Dammit." The word slipped out between his teeth. What was he supposed to do now?

Pizza? Lila turned her face toward the door of the sitting room and sniffed. Definitely pizza, pepperoni pizza, probably with green peppers and black olives. She checked her watch and wondered if she had any more of those microwave things in the freezer. Of course, even if she did, it wouldn't be hot, fresh pizza dripping with melted mozzarella and with sizzling slices of pepperoni scattered over the top. Her stomach growled, and she mentally told it to shut up and get ready for one of those frozen microwave things.

Why, tonight of all nights, did he have to bring a pizza to work? Not only was the smell bound to linger and make her own dinner even less appetizing, but as soon as he read the letter he would leave. That great-smelling pizza would be cold by the time he got home or wherever he went—which was no business of hers. The man had an ex-wife and probably a little black book of paramours, and why not? He had a lot of appeal. He was clean-cut, and good-looking in a sexy, outdoorsy kind of way. He ran a successful business with the free, independent streak of the self-employed. He worked hard and maintained high standards. He responded to ethical and moral obligations above and beyond the call of the law. The man was a paragon. There were probably a thousand other things he usually did on Friday nights, things he would prefer to do besides work on her office.

Darn it. She should have ordered her own pizza. Why didn't she think of these things in advance? And what in the world had she been working on before he'd disrupted her concentration—as he always did. She flipped through her legal pads and darned him again for being the cause of her computerless status. She wished he'd hurry up and read the letter and leave, so she could get on with her own boring dinner and boring evening.

The unmistakable sound of his hammer halted her in mid-flip. Now what was he doing? she wondered, lifting her head in irritation and letting the page fall back into place. She swiveled her chair around to listen, and her irritation increased. His hammer kept up a steady beat. He'd missed the letter.

After a minute the hammering stopped. Lila held her breath, waiting for the sound of tool gathering and door closing. She waited and waited for a span of eternity before her patience broke.

She pushed out of her chair and headed for the door. That was the worst thing about living alone, she thought. You had to do everything yourself. Now, instead of the quiet civility of a letter, she'd have to confront him with his termination. She'd be darned if she apologize in person for the near slap, though. He could read that part later.

Her steps carried her resolutely to the kitchen, where the intensifying aroma of hot pizza and a weakening will made her falter. She was too hungry for confrontation, or so she told herself, and began to turn around.

The barely audible sound of swearing stopped her. She took a few more steps toward the open doorway and stood in the middle of the kitchen, craning her neck to the left to see into the office.

As she'd thought, he was reading the letter and didn't look any too pleased with it. He was sitting in profile to her, huddled over the space heater on a stool he'd obviously just knocked together out of the scrap pile. A trouble light dangled from an open beam, casting him in a halo of illumination—him, the pizza, and the letter that held his utmost attention. He was staring at the piece of paper like a man searching for something he'd never find.

She took two more steps forward, watching in growing curiosity as he set a half-eaten piece of pizza back in the box and used his free hand to follow along with the words she'd written. Her brow furrowed, and she took another step. His action struck a strange chord in her memory. It seemed out of place, somehow wrong—until he began to whisper.

Shock stopped her in her tracks. She knew exactly where she'd seen a similar scene. It had been during one of her education practicums for her bachelor degree. She'd taught in an junior high school, the eighth grade, and a few of the children had been behind in their reading skills. The slowest of them had resorted to mouthing syllables and using his fingers to guide his eyes across the page.

Jack Hudson had the same problem. He couldn't read.

Four

The conclusion had no sooner registered in Lila's mind than Jack looked up and caught her staring at him. She blushed, and worse, she thought he did too.

Silence stretched between them, thickening the air with embarrassment and, on her part, guilt. She'd written the letter out of cowardice and had ended up putting both of them in a terribly awkward position. When would she learn to face her problems head-on?

Illiteracy. The word popped into her mind and her blush deepened. She felt ashamed for him and knew she had no right. Illiteracy conjured up conditions like poverty, below-average intelligence, and laziness—none of which applied to the Jack Hudson she knew.

She didn't know what to do. Turning around and leaving would be incredibly rude, unbearably cowardly, and would get her nowhere. He might or might not figure out that she'd meant him to be the one to leave. But staring at him didn't seem to be doing them any good either.

"Pizza?" he asked, reaching for the box on the heater, his voice gruff.

"What?" she choked out.

He cleared his throat and looked up at her. "Pizza. I brought a large one, in case you hadn't had your dinner yet."

"Oh."

"Have you?"

"What?"

"Had your dinner?"

"No." The truth was out before she thought to lie.

"Good." A grin teased the corner of his mouth. "I hate to eat alone."

She didn't know what motivated her more—relief from the overbearing tension, the opportunity to ignore what she'd just seen, the pizza, or the temptation of his smile. Whichever it was, she practically stumbled over herself jumping at his offer. "Should I get a couple of plates?"

"That'd be great. I brought a salad from Rudi's."

Her hunger shot up a degree or two, and she couldn't keep the hopefulness out of her voice. "With gorgonzola dressing?"

His grin broadened. "A pint of it."

She gave him a hesitant smile of her own, pleased with his choice, but was still feeling rocked by her discovery. *Jack Hudson couldn't read.*

All through dinner he kept the conversation going with stories about jobs he and Smitty had done. There was the one about the lady who wanted twenty built-in mannequin heads in her closet to store her wigs. The sight was so eerie, Smitty had refused to go anywhere near the bedroom. Or so Jack had thought, until he went into the huge closet one day and all the heads simultaneously jerked around toward him, their sightless eyes pinning him in front of the pile of cedar drawers he'd been working on.

"I broke two of the drawers and banged the hell out of my head on a shelf trying to get out of that closet." His laughter underscored every word. "Practically gave myself a concussion."

Lila giggled along with him, wondering if two beers were possibly one too many. She'd brought the plates out to the office, and they were both sitting around the space heater, eating pizza and salad. It was kind of like camping out, and the most unusual thing she'd done in a long time.

He grinned and twisted the top off another bottle of beer for himself. "Damn Smitty. We lost over two hundred dollars on the closet alone, but it was worth every penny. Lord, we must have laughed for a month. Every time I looked at him, he'd jerk his head around and stare at me, wide-eyed."

Lila chuckled and wiped her eyes with the red bandanna he offered, forgetting, for the moment, her own complaints against Dale Smith.

"Of course, I got him back," Jack said.

"Of course." She hiccuped.

"I found this old stuffed cobra one day down in Denver. It was all coiled up, the hood flattened out, and it was kind of wobbly. So I brought it home, and the next day, just before quitting time, I put it in the front seat of Smitty's pickup."

Lila started laughing again, and he joined in.

"I wish I'd had a camera when he opened up his truck. The look on his face. And talk about lightning reflexes. Man, he slammed that door shut so fast and so hard, he broke all the glass in the window."

Her sides were going to split; she was sure of it. His stories were crazy, absurd, and the funniest things she'd heard since she didn't know when. Imagine, mannequins coming to life and cobras on the plains of Colorado. She barely got herself under control when he added, "I've still got the snake." She burst out laughing all over again.

He rose to his feet and brushed a light kiss on the top of her head. "If you'll make some coffee, I'll get dessert."

His action surprised her, warmed her, and squelched her laughter in the blink of an eye. "Okay," she managed to say, and stood up too.

The coffee was beginning to drip when he came into the kitchen with a gold box tied with a black ribbon. The name Justine Chocolatier was inscribed across the top in black ink. Lila took one look at the box, one look at him, and said in a disbelieving voice, "You bought a whole torte?" Justine's desserts were famous over half of northern Colorado.

"The whole thing," he said. "Kahlua truffle."

"Wow," she said softly. The thought of so much decadence was a little overwhelming.

He sliced them each a generous piece, and Lila poured the coffee into two deep mugs. At his request they returned to the office, which Lila had to admit was acquiring a cozy ambience. The space heater glowed and emitted enough warmth to take the bite but not the adventure out of the air. Jack had folded his ski jacket and put it on a low stack of lumber for her to sit on, and the expanse of windows revealed a new snowstorm rolling in over the mountains.

"I'll never be able to eat all this," she said after three glorious bites.

"I know," he said with a sly twinkle in his eye. "I planned on making the ultimate sacrifice and finishing your piece after mine. That's why I made the pieces so big."

She almost asked him where it all went. Justine's Kahlua truffle torte had about one million five hundred calories per cubic inch, and he had no discernible extra weight on his tall, broad-shouldered body—his perfectly proportioned, quintessentially masculine, tall, broad-shouldered body. But on second thought, she decided such a question was far too personal and probably flirtatious. She took a sip of coffee instead and sat back to watch him eat her dessert.

He was solid. She remembered that from when he'd held her. Solid, and hard, and strong. She liked the way he smelled too. No cologne, just an enticing scent of man and sawdust. Another thought brought a private flush to her cheeks. She liked the way he tasted. She liked it a lot.

It was kind of musky, very real, and definitely erotic, especially when he cupped her face in his palm and turned her deeper into his kiss. She couldn't forget how that had felt, or the flavor he'd left in her mouth, or the textures of his tongue and teeth. The memories had kept her awake most every night of the week.

"Second to the last bite," he said, lifting his fork.

She opened her mouth and took the offered

confection. It was rich and bittersweet, smooth and heavy, divine even, but it wasn't as good as Jack Hudson's kiss.

He slowly withdrew the fork from her mouth and ate the last bite, all the while watching her until she felt a rise in her body temperature. For a moment she was afraid she might do something terrible, or wonderful, like lean closer and kiss him. She didn't think he'd mind, not when he looked at her as if he thought she, too, would taste better than Justine's Kahlua truffle torte.

When Lila gazed at him like that, Jack knew he had to get out of there before he did something he might not be able to control, like lean over and kiss her. But his curiosity insisted on knowing what was in the letter before he left. He didn't want to go home alone and struggle with her scrunched-up loops and waves, and he didn't feel like driving over to his sister's and having her read whatever Lila had written to him. That was assuming, of course, that even his sister could decipher the lady's scrawl.

"I would have done better if you'd printed," he said, allowing himself to lean forward partway. He rested his forearms on his thighs and folded his hands together so he'd know exactly where they were.

"Hmmm?" she replied.

"If you'd printed, or typed, I would have done better. Cursive always throws me, and yours is worse than most."

"Oh." Lila straightened and brushed her cheek with her hand, as if that would ease the heat left by his gaze. She knew how sloppy her handwriting was, more than one student had griped about it.

"Yes, well, if I'd known . . . known that . . ." Her voice trailed off, and the heat returned to her cheeks in full measure.

"Known that I have trouble reading," he prompted.

"Well, yes, then of course I would have printed." Lies, all lies. It she'd known how much difficulty he had reading, she wouldn't have written him a letter, period. The subject was proving to be painful, and she wished he hadn't brought it up. She wasn't sure why the subject distressed her, but figured it had a little to do with her guilt and a lot to do with being attracted to him. It somehow seemed more sexual than sensible for an English professor to be attracted to a man who either didn't or couldn't read.

She wished he wasn't funny, nice, and sexy. She wished she didn't like him, and Lord knew she was trying hard not to. After all, she thought she had learned her lesson about getting involved with inappropriate men.

Not that he was actually inappropriate, she corrected herself. She hoped she wasn't that much of a snob. But it did reinforce her belief that she and Jack Hudson had virtually nothing in common.

"Well, yes," she began, "about the letter . . ." Now she had to tell him not to come back. She took the letter he handed her and snapped it open, as if she needed reminding of what she'd written. "Well, it starts with an apology." Another lie. She'd put the apology at the end.

"For what?"

"For almost slapping you," she said, keeping her gaze glued to the page.

"Apology accepted."

"Then there's another part . . . hmmm . . ." She let her gaze skim the tersely worded phrases. "It's about what a nice job you've done on the office."

"Compliment accepted."

She could feel his grin, but she didn't look up. She didn't know why she was embarrassed, and she didn't know why she was having such a difficult time admitting to what she'd written. It had all made perfect sense at the time.

"Anything else?" he asked.

She made a big show of checking the letter front and back. "Uh . . . no, I don't think so."

"Liar."

Her head snapped up at his softly spoken accusation, her face instantly aflame. "What do you mean?"

"I'm dyslexic, Lila," he said, reaching out to brush her cheek with his thumb. "Not stupid."

Her skin burned under his touch. "There are a lot of new teaching methods for—"

"No," he gently interrupted.

"If you were tested. I mean, dyslexia can be—"

"No." His thumb slid downward and caressed her mouth, effectively silencing her.

He was going to kiss her, she knew, and there didn't seem to be anything she could do about it except wait, and lose herself in the depths of his eyes, growing languid with sensuality. She felt the heat of his body, the warmth of his breath, the unhesitating destination of his thoughts, and her lips parted.

She was sweet anticipation rising to his need, and Jack wanted the moment to last—because it wasn't going to go any further. He traced her full lower lip with the pad of his thumb, reveling in its softness, well aware of what he was passing up.

When her thick black lashes drifted down to rest on her rose-tinged cheeks, though, his resistance slipped along with intentions. He pressed his mouth against her temple, inhaling her fragrance and feeling her soft sigh blow across his face. Rationalizing that there was a difference between a kiss and a *kiss*, he decided to explore the limits of the former.

He caressed the side of her face with his mouth, following a lazy trail to the sweet patch of skin between her ear and throat. He lingered there, nuzzling—but not kissing; grazing the tenderness of her lobe with his teeth—but not kissing; tracing the curve of her jaw with his tongue—but not kissing; until he admitted her lie was nothing compared to his own. He could kiss her until he lost his mind and ever once come near her lips.

"You can keep your secrets and your letter, Lila," he murmured against her cheek. "And the torte."

Lila felt his smile before he straightened up on his makeshift stool.

"I think I'll call it a night, if that's okay with you," he continued, rising to his feet. "I need to help my dad with his barn tomorrow during the day, but I'll be back tomorrow night to finish the electrical work. I'll try to get the drywallers in here by the end of the week."

"I—I won't be here tomorrow night," she said, still breathless from whatever it was he'd been doing to her neck.

"Well, it's a small house." He grinned. "We're bound to run into each other sooner or later."

He was leaving, she thought, which was what she'd wanted. And he was coming back, which hadn't been in her plan at all. But she'd had her chance to tell him the truth about the letter, and she'd declined.

"Thank you for dinner," she said. "It was wonderful."

"Rudi's makes a helluva pizza," he agreed.

She'd been talking about his company, but she decided not to tell him that either. In fact, she needed to think before she said anything else. She'd never known a man to turn her around with such ease. She'd had everything planned before he'd shown up, and her everything had been completely flip-flopped, and the only thing that bothered her was that she wasn't bothered. Stranger things had happened, she was sure, but she couldn't remember the last time they'd happened to her.

"Well, good night," she said.

"Yeah, good night."

It was another perfect opportunity for a kiss, a classic opportunity, time-tested and practically foolproof, and they both knew it. Lila caught his quick glance at her mouth, and Jack saw her wet lips.

"Yeah, well, good night," he said again, backing toward the French doors, his voice a shade rougher than it had been.

She waved to him twice before he got into his truck, and once more as he drove down the driveway. All three times, in her private heart of hearts, she wished he weren't leaving.

Five

Another week, another plan. Lila had decided the only sensible thing left to do was to face her attraction for Jack Hudson head-on. Ignoring it certainly hadn't worked. She needed to stop thinking of him as an intriguing, unknown quantity in her life and instead put him in a new category, one she'd had years of practice controlling. She needed to make a student out of him, so she decided to teach him how to read.

Of course, she still could have just gotten rid of him. Four things kept her from doing that. She now knew where his unsettling look of defeat had come from the day he'd stood in her sitting room and stared at Danny's photograph. Dyslexics faced thousands of failures before adulthood, though she had to admit Jack Hudson seemed to have bounced back from them in pretty good shape. She didn't know exactly what had caused his resigned expression at that moment, but she didn't want to add to his score sheet of failures.

His blush had definitely swayed her. He hadn't liked being found out, but neither had he done anything to hide his disability, which led to reason number three—his mixture of courage and confidence. It took both to invite an English professor to eat pizza with you after she'd just found you sounding-out syllables.

Reason number four was self-serving and practical. Jack Hudson was the best carpenter in northern Colorado. Long after the rest of her Victorian farmhouse crumbled into dust, her office would be standing on the edge of the cornfields. She didn't doubt it for a minute.

Therefore, she'd compiled a good, solid beginning reading list. She'd take him through some of her childhood favorites, and at the end of each lesson she'd read to him from the classics. She'd give him the world.

It never occurred to her that he might not want to.

"No." Jack whacked the nail again, though he'd already sunk it an eighth of an inch past the board. He was standing with his back to her, inside the open framework of a storage closet they'd decided to add to her office.

"No?"

"No." He set another nail, and his hammer rang out.

Lila dragged her gaze from the curve of his backside, noting how nicely he fit into a pair of softly worn denims, and looked down at her cherished copy of Mother Goose. She admitted he might have a point. Maybe nursery rhymes weren't the best place to start. She'd thought the easy rhyme scheme would act as a natural prompter, whereas she'd given little thought to the subject matter.

"Okay," she conceded. "What would you like to read?"

"Nothing."

For a woman who had spent some of the best hours of her childhood on *Treasure Island* and bawling her eyes out over *The Yearling,* his answer bordered on incomprehensible.

"That's impossible," she said.

He just kept hammering away, nail after nail, whack after whack. Outside, the wind whipped up flurries of snow in the dark, blowing them off the roof of the milkhouse and scraping them across the icy crust covering the yard.

"Maybe if you told me what you were interested in," she said, trying a new tack, "a hobby or something, I could get some books on the subject." Much to her surprise, that worked.

He stopped with his hammer raised. After a long pause he landed one final blow on the last nail, then slowly turned to face her. "I don't have much going in the hobby area, but over the last few months I have been cultivating a new interest."

If his smooth drawl and the gleam in his eye hadn't warned her, his teasing grin should have, but it didn't.

"Great." She almost sighed in relief. "What is it?"

"You." His smile broadened, and he moved a couple of steps closer in a slow, sexy swagger. "So . . . if you've got an autobiography lying around somewhere or a diary you'd be willing to share, I can guarantee you my undivided attention."

He was impossible, she thought. There was no other word for him. Impossibly aggravating, impossibly good-looking, impossibly, seductively appealing.

Deciding to build an office addition onto her house hadn't seemed like such a big deal last fall. She'd just wanted someplace to set up her computer and put her books, someplace besides the living room, the sitting room, or the kitchen, someplace besides rooms already jam-packed with Danny's exotic antiques from the four corners of the world. All she'd wanted was a room of her own for her own stuff.

What she'd gotten was Jack Hudson. What she needed was help.

"You what?" Didi Caldwell's tortoiseshell glasses slid lower on her nose, giving Lila the full benefit of her blue-eyed stare across the width of a cluttered desk.

"Mother Goose," Lila admitted for the second time. "But I immediately offered to start with something else, anything else."

"After you had already offended him," her friend added with a condemning sigh. Didi sat back in her chair and swiped ineffectually at a multitude of straying, rust-colored tendrils of hair. "Sometimes you're so smart you're dumb, Lila."

"Sometimes," she was forced to agree.

"But not often," Didi said. "What can I do to help? Do you want me to find him a real reading tutor? The public library runs a good literacy program. I'm sure they can match him up with someone."

"No, no, that's not what I had in mind," Lila said, not quite meeting Didi's gaze.

"Oh. Well, I guess I could offer him as an extra-credit project to one of my grad students. Is he willing to pay an hourly wage?"

"No. I mean, that's not what I had in mind either."

Didi leaned forward and pushed her glasses back into place. "Lila honey, I have adolescent literature, grammar, and reading for education majors this semester. There's no way I can cram an illiterate carpenter into my personal schedule."

"I'm not asking you to. I'm working him into my own schedule. I just need to know what to do. I thought you could give me a few pointers."

"Why?"

Lila frowned at the blunt question, thinking the answer was obvious. "So I don't make any more mistakes."

"That wasn't the question," her friend said, giving her a knowing look. When Lila didn't reply, Didi sighed. "Is there something about this guy I should know that you're not telling me?"

"He's a nice man," Lila hedged.

"And?"

She shifted slightly in her chair, wondering if her students felt as uncomfortable as she suddenly did on the wrong side of the desk. "And he's doing a lot of extra work on my office, and I'd like to help him out. Isn't that what teaching is all about?"

"That's what it's *supposed* to be about. That's what I tell my students it's about. But you've been in this game long enough to know it ain't necessarily so, especially at the university level. And that, my dear, is the level we are at." Didi paused long enough for her words to sink in, then asked, "What's his name?"

"Jack. Jack Hudson." Lila watched Didi's eyebrows slowly draw together. "What?"

Didi shrugged. "The name sounds familiar, but I don't know why. I've never hired a carpenter in my life, functionally illiterate or otherwise. Kevin does all our fix-it work." Kevin was Didi's husband, an art professor and no handyman, not by anyone's standards.

"Maybe you'd be better off with a carpenter," Lila said with a slight smile. "I've seen some of Kevin's carpentry. The next time he gets excited about building onto the deck, call me, and I'll give you Jack's number. He's incredible."

"Incredible?" Didi's eyebrows rose above the tortoiseshell frames, and Lila realized there had been more than a trace of enthusiasm in her voice.

"Good," she amended. "He's very good at his job."

"Oh?" Didi's eyebrows didn't budge a millimeter. "Are we talking about a good, illiterate, *old* carpenter, or a good, illiterate, prime-of-manhood carpenter?"

"Actually, he's dyslexic."

Didi gasped. "I don't believe it! You're seeing a man!"

It was a leap of logic to be sure, but Lila knew how her friend's mind worked, and she knew Didi would be hard to dissuade. Still, she had to try. She couldn't let one of her oldest and dearest friends harbor false hopes.

"I said he was dyslexic, Didi. I wasn't being evasive."

"You were being evasive, totally evasive. Of course, dyslexia is a whole different problem from functional illiteracy. You should have told me right up front. The library program is no good. Their volunteers aren't trained to tutor dyslexics. I can't wait to meet him. He must be very special. Do you know how long it's been since you had a date?" She paused as if she expected an answer, and when she didn't get one, she filled in her own blank. "A year ago December."

"Thank you, Dee," Lila drawled, "for reminding me of such a pleasant occasion." Thankfully, Didi missed the sarcasm.

"It was awful!" she exclaimed. "I was there. Remember? But a whole year, Lila? Man does not live by bread alone."

"And it's physically impossible to die of embarrassment," Lila countered, one clichéd phrase for another.

"Hey, wait a minute. You said he couldn't read the letter you'd written him?"

"Yes," she said, wary of what Didi was going to ask next.

"Handwritten?"

"Yes."

"Well, hell, Lila. *I* can't read your handwriting, and I have a doctorate."

"My handwriting is not that bad."

"It's worse," Didi said succinctly. "Bring him around to the reading lab on Wednesday, and I'll have him tested. Then we can figure out where to go from there. Okay?"

"No, not okay. He doesn't want to be tested. I'm not even sure he wants to learn how to read."

Didi thought about that for a moment, then

threw Lila another curve. "Maybe he already knows how and he just doesn't like to read. It wouldn't be on the top of a dyslexic's list of fun things to do."

Perfect, Lila thought, sinking deep into the chair. She hadn't fired him because he couldn't read, and she couldn't teach him to read because he might already know. She'd ignored him and confronted him, kissed him and offended him, lied with him and to him. She'd be darned if she knew what else to do with him.

Fortunately, Jack was full of ideas, and he wasn't shy about pursuing them.

"I've been doing some thinking," he said that evening. He'd taken a short break from working on the office, helped himself to a cup of coffee in the kitchen, then unerringly wandered into the sitting room, where Lila worked every night.

She swiveled her desk chair around at the sound of his voice, and he wondered anew at the sheer delicacy and beauty of her face. He'd never seen skin so pretty, like cream blushed with rose petals, and he knew she'd be like that all over. It was enough to drive him crazy in the dark hours of the night. He wanted to do all the things to her men did to women who made them feel the way she made him feel.

"About your offer," he explained at her expectant look.

"You mean the reading?" she asked, and he swore he heard hope and anticipation in her voice.

"Yes. I've thought it over, and if we can agree on a couple of ground rules, I think reading lessons would be a good idea." His sister, Karen, would have shot him for saying such a thing. Even after all these years, he hated to think of the many sacrifices she'd made trying to beat the difference between *b* and *d* into his brain, the missed parties, the canceled dates, the homework she hadn't had time to finish for her own classes because doing his had taken them half the night. She'd taught him how to read by a hundred methods he hoped Lila had never heard of. Being an older sister, she hadn't been above a little physical torture to get his attention back after it had wandered off in confusion. She'd pinched his arm so many times, he'd been afraid he'd never have a decent muscle, and she'd promised him she'd make sure he didn't if he didn't learn how to spell *muscle.*

Muscle. One of those words that made no phonetic sense whatsoever. What pinching hadn't accomplished, the fear of growing up to be a ninety-eight-pound weakling had. He'd learned how to spell *muscle,* and Karen had rewarded him with a set of garage sale weights.

She'd been good at rewards. There had always been brownies and cookies for his lunch, and every Sunday before church she'd fixed him and his dad a big pancake breakfast to make up for all the cold cereal during the week. He hadn't missed his mom very often, not as much as his dad, of course, or his sister, who'd had a chance to really know her before she died. Karen had made sure he felt the loss as little as possible. Once, she'd even skipped school to be a "homeroom mother" and bring cupcakes to his fifth-grade class.

And he'd just implied to Lila Singer that he didn't know how to read. He hadn't denied it before because she'd angered him with her Mother Goose book, and because she obviously hadn't believed him when he'd told her the only reason he'd had a problem with her letter was because of her handwriting. Then when she'd asked about hobbies, he hadn't been able to resist telling her what he was really interested in.

It had only been later that he'd come up with his plan. She wanted to teach him how to read, and he wanted to spend time with her. It was practically a natural—except for two tiny problems: He already knew how to read, and the time he wanted to spend with her wasn't with their noses stuck in a book of nursery rhymes.

"Ground rules?" she asked, and he took a deep breath, readying himself for his long shot.

"I pick all the reading material, and to keep this from being a charity case, I think it's important for you to let me pay you for your services."

"My services?" she repeated, looking as surprised as she sounded.

"Okay," he said quickly, lifting a hand and verbally backing off. "I know you didn't offer to help me for money, but if you won't take payment, you have to let me make it up to you somehow, maybe with dinner, like the other night."

Lila's first instinct was to say no. She wasn't helping him for any personal gain, except for that bit about demystifying his appeal, putting him in a controllable category. She'd already offended him once, though, and she didn't dare do it again, not if they were going to get their student-teacher relationship off to a good start.

"The pizza was nice," she said slowly. "I think we

can do that every now and then to keep things even."

"It won't always be pizza," he warned, and she nodded her assent.

"I'm flexible when it comes to food," she said.

In truth, since Danny's death she'd become extremely flexible. She'd eat anything she didn't have to cook first, anything the frozen food companies wanted to throw at her, anything the fast food joints could dream up.

"Great." A smile spread across his face, deepening the creases in his cheeks and lighting his eyes, and suddenly she was flustered. "I'm going to go finish the second coat of paint," he continued. "I'll get back to you later in the week about the particulars for our first lesson."

"Sure, fine." She busied herself with tidying the papers on her desk, piling Greek gods on top of Brontë sisters. "Whatever you come up with will be fine, I'm sure."

Jack knew he should be ashamed of himself, blatantly manipulating her into dinner like that—but he wasn't.

She should have been stronger, more forceful, less malleable, Lila thought. She should have stood her ground, demanded her rights, spoken up for herself.

She should have worn her black dress.

She looked around the dining room of the Cove Garden restaurant and realized it was still too close to the holidays for people to have settled back into their normal, casual attire. Nope. Women wanted one more reason to wear their finest, and in the university town that meant dinner at either the Cove Garden or Shirewood's. Jack had picked her favorite of the two, the Cove Garden with its non-nouvelle cuisine. The chef at the Cove had never stopped believing in cream and butter.

She wished he'd told her where they were going. His "let's go into town and grab a bite" fell far short of describing most excursions to the Cove. She could have worn her black dress and her mink coat. Darn him, she thought, burying her nose in the menu. She could have worn her pearls and her black suede heels. The opportunity arose so seldomly in her life. If she'd only known, she wouldn't have missed this one.

He must have known, though. The place was packed, probably requiring reservations made a week ago. A week ago? She lowered her menu a scant inch, far enough to stare at him over the top.

"You're cheating," she said without preamble.

Jack glanced up from his own menu, wondering how he'd given up the game so quickly. "I'm not reading the menu, honest."

"Of course you're not reading the menu," she said sotto voce, so as not to embarrass him. "If you could read the menu, we wouldn't be here. I mean the restaurant."

"What about the restaurant?"

"People don't 'grab a bite to eat' at the Cove Garden."

"They don't?"

"No, they don't. You 'grab a bite' at Rudi's. You 'dine' at the Cove. Knowing the correct usage of words to impart your true meaning is almost as important as knowing how to read."

"Oh."

"Oh, indeed." She stuck her nose back in the menu. "Would you like poultry or beef?"

"Beef."

"Okay." She drew the word out on a long breath, shifting her attention to the right-hand page. "They have steak au poivre, which has crushed peppercorns in it, very tasty; filet mignon wrapped in bacon; tournedos with bearnaise sauce; beef Wellington loaded with pâté de foie gras and dux-elles, or, if you prefer, filet de boeuf en croute; prime rib; and the last surviving chateaubriand west of the Mississippi."

Jack listened attentively, though he knew the menu by heart. He liked the way she pronounced the French words. He liked the way her mouth moved. He liked remembering the way her mouth had moved under his.

He sat up straighter in his chair and forced his gaze back to the leather-bound menu. "What killed off all the other chateaubriands?"

Lila glanced up, giving him a blank look. Then she bubbled into disbelieving laughter.

"Women's lib, Jack," she told him between chuckles. "Women's lib killed off the chateaubri-ands." He was crazy, and funny, and quick, and she liked him. As a matter of fact, she liked him a lot.

"Well, I'm all for the liberation of women," he said, "so I guess we'd better save this one for posterity. I'm going to have prime rib. How about you?"

"Filet de boeuf en croute," she said, looking over the menu again. Then she quickly glanced up. "Beef Wellington. Sorry. I took a minor in French as an undergrad."

"I flunked a semester of Spanish in high school."

There it was again, she thought. They had absolutely nothing in common, nothing except astounding kisses and liking each other. It wasn't enough, and it was time she made the point clear.

"I graduated summa cum laude from the University of Denver, and—and my husband was a Rhodes scholar." She rushed through the last part, unable to meet his gaze.

"He was a great photographer too," Jack said, sounding completely unimpressed by her information. "When did he die?"

"Three years ago." She picked up her napkin and concentrated on smoothing it out on her lap.

"That's a long time to be alone."

"I—I wasn't alone all the time."

If her voice had been any softer, Jack wouldn't have heard her. Truth be known, he wished he hadn't.

Six

The ritual of ordering dinner dragged on, taking longer than usual because Jack had a hard time paying attention to the waiter's questions. He had too many questions of his own running around in his brain. Questions like, If she hadn't been alone since her husband's death, who had she been with? What had happened? And where was the mystery man now?

He felt as if he'd had the rug jerked around beneath his feet, just enough to throw him off balance. He'd reconciled the facts of her marriage and widowhood with his feelings for her, and he'd staked his claim the night he'd muscled old Trey out of her house. Now there was this new guy, and from the tone of her voice he had the status of being part of a "past." Jack was curious as all get out, his mind working overtime with possibilities, and he wanted to ask questions, lots of questions. Trouble was, she'd decided to monopolize the conversation with questions of her own—although she didn't seem to be giving them her full attention.

"Have you had the prime rib here before?" she asked, not quite meeting his eyes.

"Yes, a couple of times." He paused for the buildup to his first question, but she beat him to the punch.

"Have you ever ordered the beef Wellington?"

"A couple of times. I—"

"I've always wondered how they cooked them. You know, getting the pastry and the filet to come out at the same time."

"I think they cook the filet first, then finish it off in the oven with the pastry, and I was wondering about—"

"So you're a believer in women's liberation?" she interrupted, fiddling with her napkin again, her gaze directed at her lap.

He sighed. "In theory."

Her head came up, and a spark of indignation flashed in her eyes, assuring him he'd finally gotten her attention. "What do you mean, in theory?"

"Liberation is great for anyone, but like everything else, it comes with a price. In some areas, I don't think liberation has been such a good deal for women."

"And what areas are those?" Lila asked, pressing him for an answer that she was sure would plummet him to the depths of her regard, which was the safest place for him. She didn't know what in the world had compelled her to say such a stupid thing as "I wasn't alone all the time." What was wrong with her? Did she need her head examined? She never talked about that period in her life. Never. Not with anyone.

Not until Jack Hudson had looked at her with what she considered to be a very disturbing mixture of compassion and desire. He never should have kissed her. Not the first time, the second time, or the third time, if the third time could even be called a kiss. The memory of his mouth on her cheek, her neck, her ear, still sent shivers down her spine. He definitely had a way about him.

Well, that settled it, she thought, stifling a groan and casting her eyes heavenward. *A way about him . . .* She did need her head examined.

"Well, I think it's great that women have a chance at any career they want." With effort, Lila refocused her attention on what he was saying. "And I don't know how long it will be before they get equal pay for equal work, but I think what they need just as much is an increase in appreciation for their traditional roles."

"I see." At least she thought she saw his point. She might have missed a word or two, but the parts she'd caught didn't amount to a male chauvinist jerk's opinion.

"How about you? What do you think?" he asked.

"Me?"

"Yes. What do you think of traditional roles for women?"

"I don't know," she said, rearranging her napkin yet again. "I never had one."

"You were a wife."

"Well, yes, but being the wife of Danny Singer had more to do with style than roles. He was not a traditional man."

"What kind of man was he?"

The question hung in the air, unacknowledged and unanswered. She creased the damask napkin one way and then the other, running her buffed nail across the folds in the white cloth while she debated the wisdom of opening up yet another subject for discussion with Jack. Not that she had anything to hide. Her marriage had been good, very good, something she was proud of. In truth, if she could have gotten away with it, she'd have worn a sign around her neck that said I GOT MARRIAGE RIGHT, and to hell with grammar. It was love affairs where she'd proven to be a dismal failure.

"Danny was a star, a bright, flaming star," she started to say slowly, looking up at Jack. "Living with him was like living on a nonstop roller coaster fueled by excitement. He did things with light and a camera no one else had ever dreamed of, and the world made him rich and famous. He was no saint, but for five years he was the man I loved. For five years he was the man who loved me."

Jack nodded sympathetically as he mentally kicked himself. He had to ask, hadn't he? Yes, by golly, he just had to know about Danny Singer. Past loves had never been his favorite topic of conversation with women he was dating, at least not until Lila Singer. Maybe he'd allowed himself to get rusty. He hadn't been dating much this past year. He'd been too busy, and his last blind date had been remarkably lacking in things like conversation and mutual interest.

Funny thing, though, he hadn't felt rusty when he'd kissed Lila, and even as the words "the man who loved me" fell from her lips, he wanted to kiss her again. Maybe he *was* rusty. He was beginning to suffer from a one-track mind. But then, what man wouldn't when she looked the way she did tonight?

She had on one of those soft, fuzzy sweaters again, angora or something. It was cut wide across the shoulders, revealing cream-colored skin and the delicate protrusion of her collarbone. Shiny black buttons held it together down the front, matching the rich ebony of the wool and the midnight cloud of her hair. It was the kind of sweater that invited a man's touch.

"You saw the photograph he took of me?" she asked. "The one in the sitting room?"

He nodded. Oh, yes. He saw it in his sleep.

"He created the lighting effects on location, not in the darkroom. No one has been able to duplicate them. Did you notice the way my skin glowed?"

He nodded again. He'd noticed, especially in the curve of her neck and the slope of her shoulder. He'd noticed it in the satin slide of skin from beneath her breast to over her hip. He'd noticed it in the sleek straightaway of her thigh.

"I can't tell you how many people have come to me and asked me to tell them how he did it."

Jack cleared his throat. "How did he do it?"

A surprisingly mischievous smile lit her face, curving her lush, full mouth, and she leaned closer over the table. "Nobody believes me, but I don't know. I saw the umbrellas and the filters, and all the strobe equipment, but I don't know how he made them work together. He made only two hundred prints, and the last I heard they were going for five thousand on the open market. Five thousand dollars for a bit of light magic."

No, Jack thought, not five thousand for a bit of

light magic. Five thousand for her, for the magic of Lila Singer wrapped in gauze and moonbeams.

Dinner came and dinner went, and Jack barely tasted a bite. He hadn't tried to work the conversation around to whoever had been holding her hand since Danny's death. He wasn't up to another rundown of virtues, and vices would be even worse.

When dinner was over, he paid the check with his credit card and managed to keep from wincing when she commended his signature on the slip.

"That's very good, Jack."

"Thank you. I practice."

In his truck, driving home, she glanced at one of the books he'd brought for them to read. He'd conveniently turned on the dome light for her.

"*Welding from A to Z and Beyond*?" she read the title aloud.

"You said hobbies."

"Doesn't sound like much of a hobby," she murmured, envisioning bumpers and ball jacks.

"It's all in the wrist."

She hid a quick grin and glanced over at him. He said the craziest things. And he was cute. Well, maybe not cute exactly, but cute seemed a safer adjective than the naked truth.

Naked? Oh, great, now she'd really gone too far. She shouldn't even be thinking about things like Jack Hudson without his clothes on, or Jack Hudson's chest, how the silky mat of hair would feel sliding between her fingers, how soft his skin would be, how hard the muscle beneath. How it would feel to press her mouth to the tender part of his throat and have his arms encircle her and hold her tight against all his . . . nakedness.

She shifted slightly, a weak-hearted attempt to put more distance between them, then forced herself to look out the windshield instead of at his face, which wasn't cute at all, but sexy like the rest of him. It was in his eyes, the curve of his eyebrows, the sweep of his hair off his forehead. *Sexy* described his mouth, and his shoulders, and his hands. It was the first word she'd thought of when he'd stood in her doorway at six o'clock that evening in his pleated canvas slacks, black polo shirt, braided leather belt, and bomber jacket. It had been the second word to cross her mind when he'd smiled his slightly off-center smile and looked at her with an appreciative twinkle in his eye.

She'd thought it half a dozen more times as he suggested dinner before reading lessons, and she'd had to force herself not to gaze too long at either his mouth or his eyes, or any other part of him, all of which seemed to fascinate her beyond the bounds of reason.

With a silent sigh she closed her eyes and lifted a gloved hand to her brow. Her plan wasn't working. Against all of her saner instincts, she continued to be attracted to him, and attracted was putting it mildly. She didn't know how he'd slipped into her life and her imagination, but he'd become a permanent fixture in both. He'd certainly done nothing overt, except for those kisses. Maybe that was all it had taken. She hadn't been kissed in a long time, and though she didn't subscribe to the "sex is a necessary part of life" theory, she knew Jack's kiss had touched her more than physically.

Another sigh escaped her. She shifted again in her seat and kept watching the darkness roll by until she saw the silhouette of her house against the sky.

The night stretched over the prairie in all its icy clarity, leaving the barest path open for a silvery stream of moonlight to filter down through the cottonwoods bordering her driveway. The hinges on the truck doors creaked in frozen protest as they opened them. Lila didn't wait for him to come around to help her, a subtle way of letting him know she didn't consider their night out a date. She couldn't afford to, no matter how expensive and wonderful dinner had been.

Once inside, he offered to build a fire in her living room fireplace, and she asked him if he'd like cream and sugar with his coffee.

"No," he said. "Black is fine."

One mistake after another, she thought, walking into the kitchen. One lousy mistake after another. She had a furnace, and it worked fine. They didn't need a cozy, romantic fire to study.

They didn't need Irish cream in their coffee either, but she poured a good dollop into each steaming mug, then arranged a variety of fancy cookies on a silver tray. Her lipstick was probably fine, too, but she checked it in her compact mirror just in case. Just in case of what, she wasn't sure. It was a purely precautionary measure.

He had a perfect fire going when she returned to the living room, perfect like the breadth of his shoulders in relation to the length of his torso, perfect like the stretch of fabric outlining his thigh as he knelt on the hearth, adding the last log. He wasn't overly muscular, he was just right. Perfect, from the tracing of veins up the inside curve of his arm to the hard swell of bicep showing below the short sleeve of his shirt.

Short sleeves in winter, she thought with a forced huff, trying to construe his choice as a fashion blunder. But nothing that looked as good as that shirt did on him could ever be a fashion blunder, and he gave no signs of being chilled. Quite the contrary. When he looked over his shoulder and smiled at her, she felt the temperature in the room rise a good ten degrees, enough to make undoing the first two buttons on her sweater seem like a wise decision—until she did it. The responsive widening of his eyes made her face flame with the realization of what she'd done.

"It's a little warm in here, don't you think?" She stumbled through her excuse, hardly buying it herself.

"Pretty warm," he agreed with a grin. "And getting warmer."

She smiled wanly and settled herself on the couch, directing her attention to the books he'd brought in from the truck. She assumed *Welding from A to Z and Beyond* would be her last choice, and she set it aside. Sixty excruciatingly silent seconds later she picked it up and looked at it with renewed interest.

He'd brought another book, one more, a work of fiction the likes of which she'd seen but never read. She'd noticed her students reading books similar to the one he'd brought, her female students. Her mother read them too. A year ago, even Didi had pressed one into her hands and said, "You've got to read this!" but Lila had never felt an equal sense of urgency. The book had disappeared in her library somewhere, and she didn't think this was the time to initiate herself into the world of historical romantic fiction. Not with Jack looking over her shoulder, and not if the cover was any indication of what they'd find inside *Night of the Hawk.*

She had a few jocks in her literature classes from time to time, young men who gloried in their own physiques. She'd seen enough torn T-shirts revealing rock-hard abdomens, and bulging biceps showing below frayed sleeves to last her a lifetime, or at least until next semester. She wasn't a prude, but she'd never been able to appreciate a good, solid muscle without a brain behind it.

The Hawk looked plenty smart, and the rough clothing covering him allowed enticing glimpses of a man's, not a boy's, muscled body. His long seal-brown hair was tied at his nape, a few strands left free to frame a chiseled face that spoke of the power and dignity of a warrior-king. Moonlight streamed over his tall frame, shadowing the tough leanness of his body. His clothes were colored like the horizon behind him, in shades of ice gray to match his eyes.

That was what had taken her sixty seconds, that and the way he was looking at the woman in his arms. The artist had captured a special tenderness in his gaze, a fierce tenderness. One look convinced Lila he'd lay down his life for his woman, and that's what the cover said. In every ancient, primitive way imaginable, she was the Hawk's woman. The cascade of tawny blond hair flowing across her bare shoulders was gathered in his fist. His other arm held her around the waist in a protective, possessive gesture. She was looking off into the distance, but he was looking at her, unfailing.

Welding from A to Z and Beyond had an arc welder on the cover with an interesting spray of sparks zipping off into the corners of the book. But that wasn't the only interesting thing about it.

She opened the book and read a much more interesting item on the flyleaf: *To Jack with love. Happy Birthday, Karen.*

She stared at the handwriting—printing, actually—for a moment, then asked very nonchalantly, "When was your birthday?"

"Last week," he said, coming over and sitting down beside her.

"Oh."

"The book was a present from my sister."

"Oh," she said again, relieved, but thinking a book was a particularly poor gift for someone who couldn't read. What had his sister been thinking? Especially a "with love" sister.

"She's the one who sent along the other book too," Jack said. "She was afraid you might find welding a little dry." Karen had also thought it was about time her brother showed more than a passing interest in a woman. Rather than being displeased with his inability to read ploy, she'd told him he could always use the practice, since he did tend to avoid the written word, and she'd rummaged under her bed until she'd found the perfect primer. "No woman can resist this man," she'd told him with an uncomfortably dreamy sigh. Uncomfortable, that is, for Jack. He'd told his sister he had plenty of competition, thank you, and did she have another book. She'd only said, "Trust me."

"Actually," Lila said, "I think *Welding from A to Z*

and Beyond is going to better suit our purposes."
She opened the handbook to the first chapter and
tried to keep her gaze off the cover of the romance
novel. The Hawk looked like Jack with a wild
streak, and she didn't need the added stimulation
to her imagination. "Do you know the alphabet?"

"Inside out and backward," he said, grinning.

She slanted him a wry glance. "Dyslexic joke?"

He laughed and helped himself to a handful of
cookies.

Five minutes later Lila realized there was more
to welding than she'd thought, and most of it was
couched in technical jargon. Boring, indecipher-
able technical jargon. She was halfway through
the book and she still hadn't found a good starting
page. She never should have agreed to let him
bring his own material, she thought, or allowed
him to sit quite so close to her on the couch. He
disrupted her concentration.

"Stop," he suddenly said, scooting even closer
and making it difficult for her even to breathe.
"Back up a couple of pages. Yep. That's it. That's
the page we want."

"Arc, TIG, MIG?"

"Just the arc part. I don't need TIG capabilities
or MIG speed."

"How lovely," she mumbled, searching the page
for something simple, something she understood
and he could read.

"I'm not even sure I need arc," he added.

Then why, she asked silently, was she reading
stuff like, "The duty cycle at nonrated amperage is
inversely proportional to the square of the new
amperage?" She'd always struggled with anything
remotely related to mathematics, but she kept her

thoughts to herself and scanned farther down the page.

"Okay," she finally said. "Here's a good sentence to start with." She set her finger on the page below a line of type. He leaned over her, and she swore she could feel his body heat warming her right side.

"AC or DC?"

"Yes, that's the one. Can you read it?"

He dutifully repeated the line. "AC or DC, but that's no sentence, teach."

"Hmm?" She jerked her head up and her gaze collided with his sexy grin.

"No verb."

"Oh. Of course." He had the most interesting mouth, she mused, and she liked the way it curved higher on one side when he smiled. She liked remembering how it had felt to have his mouth on hers. She'd liked everything about his kiss . . . the heat, the taste, the sensation he'd aroused deep in her breast. She slowly lifted her gaze to meet his and swallowed.

Jack knew an invitation when he saw one, and invitation was melting in her brown eyes. Color raced across her cheeks, flushing her skin rose-petal pink. If he had thought before he acted, he might have decided not to kiss her, because kissing her wasn't likely to lead where he'd want to go. But he was only a man—and damn glad of it.

He raised his hand to her face and brushed his thumb across her skin from the corner of her mouth to below her cheekbone. As her eyes drifted closed, he kept his hand moving, until his fingers tunneled through the heavy richness of her ebony curls and his palm cupped the nape of her neck.

Then, before he lowered his mouth to hers, he let his gaze roam down her silky throat to where she'd unbuttoned the two buttons, and he wished she'd freed two more.

He made no preliminary passes when he kissed her. He covered her mouth with his, and the slow stroke of his tongue across her lips granted him immediate access to her honeyed sweetness. Her response was instantaneous, and arousal raced between them like a flash fire.

Welding from A to Z and Beyond fell to the floor with an unheeded clunk. He wanted to touch her. He wanted to lower her to the couch and press into her. He thought they'd gotten kissing down to a fever pitch and it was time to move on. She was doing things with her mouth he never wanted to stop, not when they seemed to pull on his loins. She was sweet, so sweet, and he wanted all of her. He slid his other hand up to her breast and groaned deep in his throat.

Shimmering waves of excitement flooded through Lila at that sound and his caress. Oh, yes, Jack definitely had a way about him, a way of making her feel her power as a woman, and it turned her senses to putty. The gentle, insistent strength of him, his easy, seductive aggression, became more and more irresistible with each track of his mouth over hers, with each—

"Lila? Lila, honey? Are you home?"

Her mother? In the kitchen? At eight-thirty on a Saturday night?

"I knocked, honey, but you didn't answer, so I let myself in. I brought food." Cupboard doors opened and closed.

"My . . . my mother," she gasped, but he captured her mouth again, and she sank under the spell of yet one more kiss.

"I'm putting soup in the freezer and spaghetti sauce in the refrigerator to thaw. Don't worry. I brought some pasta too."

Her mother was in the kitchen, and she was in the living room kissing the living daylights out of Jack Hudson and enjoying every forbidden second, every single sensation.

"Whose truck is that in the driveway, Lila?" a masculine voice asked, and Lila froze.

Her father? In the kitchen? With her mother?

"My . . . my father," she muttered against Jack's mouth.

Now, deep in the heart of every male member of the species is a special spot saved for the fear and respect of fathers of daughters, especially fear and respect of fathers of daughters they're kissing, *especially* if in their hearts and minds they're fast moving far beyond the kissing stage.

"Your father?" he whispered, stealing more kisses from the corner of her mouth, the curve of her cheek, and the wonderful spot he'd found on the side of her neck, just below her left ear, which seemed to drive her a little bit crazy.

"My sweater!" she exclaimed softly, wondering how in the world he'd gotten her unbuttoned to the point of revealing her bra. He nipped at her neck, and she moaned, her fingers fumbling with the shiny black circles of plastic.

"Say hello to your dad," he instructed her, kissing her again and taking over the buttoning job.

"Hi, Dad!" she hollered breathlessly, and thought if that didn't bring him running, nothing would.

"Tell him we're in the living room."

"I—I can't tell him that."

"Tell him." He pressed a kiss beneath her collarbone and silently cursed parental timing.

Jack was undermining her breathing faculties, Lila thought, let alone her speaking faculties, but she managed to get the words out. "We're in the living room!"

"We picked you up a trunk at an auction today," her father called back, still in the kitchen and mercifully not charging into the living room. "Should I put it in the office? Hey, this place is looking great. Didn't I tell you Hudson would make good on the job?"

Make good? Lila repeated silently. Her father didn't know the half of what Jack Hudson could make good.

"Honey," her mother added, "I'm putting the canned jams in the cupboard and the refrigerator jams in the refrigerator."

"Thanks," she whispered. She was buttoned. Her hair was smoothed back into place. He'd stopped kissing her. She felt absolutely bereft and she wondered why.

"You're welcome." Jack stood up and ran a quick hand through his own hair before moving over to sit on the hearth. She was going to be the death of him.

Approaching footsteps sent them both into action, Lila picking up a book, and Jack putting another log on the fire.

"Well, hey, Janie, look who's here!" Lila's father spoke first. "I thought I recognized your truck, Jack. The deck still looks great."

"Glad to hear it, sir." Jack extended his hand for

a hearty shake. He remembered the couple well, Kurt and Janie Davis. Lila got her coloring from her father, a big, dark-haired man in his late fifties with a perpetual smile and a helluva handshake.

"We're thinking about adding a gazebo in the spring," her mother said, and Jack knew exactly where Lila had gotten her delicate bone structure and the sweet, breathless quality in her voice. "Do you do gazebos?"

"Sure do. I even have a few designs of my own. If you like, I can send you some pictures."

"That would be lovely." Janie turned to her daughter. "What are you reading, dear?"

Lila glanced down at the book in her hands, and for a fleeting second wondered if dyslexia was catching. She didn't recognize a single word. Her mother quickly cured her momentary confusion.

"Maybe if you turned it around. I think I recognize the cover."

Lila blushed. She didn't need to turn it around. There were only two books in the living room, and *Welding from A to Z and Beyond* was still on the floor.

"*Night of the Hawk*," her mother read, tilting her honey-blond head far to one side. "I loved that book. I'm so glad to see you're doing a little recreational reading, something relaxing. Although, if I recall correctly, this one is more exciting than relaxing." She lifted the book out of her daughter's hand and turned it right side up. "Oh, my, yes," she murmured. "I remember this man."

Lila's blush deepened, but fortunately her father and Jack were well into a conversation about redwood and gazebos—a conversation Jack was destined to end the evening with. After half an hour of two-by-fours and lattices, he conceded a silent victory to Lila's father. There was no getting rid of the man, and he knew why. His daughter looked kissed.

Jack had done his best, both in kissing her and in trying to disguise the fact, but even thirty minutes later she still looked kissed and softly mussed. Her skin was flushed, her mouth swollen, and most damning of all, he'd missed a button. Her father wasn't leaving, no way.

Jack kept up his end of the chitchat for another fifteen minutes, holding out for a miracle before he finally gave up. He extricated himself from the gazebo dream and shook hands all around, holding on to Lila's hand as he finished his good-byes.

"Nice seeing you both again," he said to her parents. "Be sure to get in touch when you're ready to start building." He took a step backward, pulling Lila with him toward the kitchen and giving her father a look that said, *Okay, you win, but I'm taking five minutes. Relax. Nothing can happen in five minutes.* All the while he was wondering what he could fit into five minutes of semi-privacy at her back door.

"I'm sorry about the lesson," she said when they were out of earshot and eyesight.

"We'll do better next time," he said with a grin, slipping into his jacket, then grasping her hands in his.

She didn't resist when he placed her palms on either side of his waist, or when he draped his arms over her shoulders and drew her against his chest. She felt so right, so good. He kissed the top of her head and tightened his arms around her. He wished he were taking her home with him, home to where there weren't any mothers and fathers.

The way she held him made him think she wished the same. Her cheek rested against his chest. Her arms had slid around his waist.

"I'm falling in love with you," he murmured against her hair, and even as he registered surprise at the words coming out of his mouth, he rejoiced in the slight tightening of her arms. He placed a kiss on her temple and felt her sigh. "I want you, Lila." His voice grew huskier. "Anytime, anyplace, anyway I can get you. Call me."

Seven

Anytime? Anyplace?

Lila thumped her pillow and threw herself down on the bed. What kind of thing was that to say? And the bit about falling in love. What did he mean by that?

She hit the pillow again. She was supposed to be teaching him to read. He was supposed to be building her an office. They were not supposed to end up in a breathtaking clinch every time they were alone for more than three minutes.

They had something going. There was no denying it, and it wasn't a client-contractor relationship, or a teacher-student relationship. It was a relationship-relationship, the last thing on earth she'd been looking for in her life.

They'd had a date, complete with good-night kiss. He'd taken her out to the fanciest restaurant in town. She'd invited him in for coffee—with Irish cream no less—and they'd ended up on the couch with her sweater partially unbuttoned.

She groaned and buried her head in her much-molested pillow. What made Jack Hudson so damned irresistible? His smile? His eyes? His body? She squeezed her eyes shut and thought for a moment. He had a great body, which was not exactly the revelation of the century, but there was more, much more, to the man.

Looking at the facts, he seemed no more than average. Brown hair, hazel eyes, six feet tall, self-employed carpenter. The most unusual thing about him, his dyslexia, wasn't what she'd call an asset.

Yet the man remained special, and it came from deep inside him. His offhand remarks made her laugh. His kisses made her melt. The best thing about his great body wasn't how it looked, but how she felt when he held her in his arms. She felt excitement, to be sure, but she also felt comfort. She didn't understand it. He didn't read books, and his idea of a good time was welding. What in the world would they do after making love?

Who cares? a little voice asked.

"I do," she whispered. She wouldn't allow herself to make another mistake out of loneliness.

Sighing, she rolled onto her back and stared at the ceiling. Everything had been so easy with Danny, so simple. They'd met, fallen instantly in love in one of those classic "eyes meeting across a crowded room" scenes, and been married inside of two months. Everything had been perfect, until he'd died in a stupid car crash.

It had taken her years to forgive him for leaving her alone. She hadn't thought it possible to love someone and yet hate him, to be so angry and full of despair all at the same time. Some nights she'd wanted him back just so she could yell at him. Most nights she'd wanted him back just so she could hold him and be held by him . . . held by him the way Jack had held her that very night when he'd whispered he was falling in love.

It was impossible. Lust she could accept, maybe. Affection and attraction were reasonable. But love was what she'd had with Danny. Love was what she'd fooled herself into believing she might have had a year earlier, before the dream had been shattered at the Silver Bell Ball.

Lila knew she'd have to step back into the man-woman stream sooner or later. She didn't see herself alone for the rest of her life. But her emotions and her pride still smarted from the memories of the Silver Bell Ball.

The night had been magical, filled with holiday spirit and good tidings. The man escorting her had been classically handsome, exceptionally intelligent, wildly successful, and, much to her disbelieving surprise, married. The wife, understandably, had looked a little haggard by the time she'd tracked her wayward spouse to the Washington Center, site of the annual Silver Bell Ball, but then, she'd come a long way on a snowy night, and Lila suspected she'd been drinking.

Three weeks of illusory bliss had come to a screeching halt among all the glitter, dazzle, and silver papier-mâché bells hanging in the lobby. Mrs. Robert Stanford, wife of the distinguished engineer who'd been called in to consult on a NASA project being researched at the university, wife of the handsome, intelligent, successful, conniving, low-down jerk holding Lila's arm, had all but ripped Lila's dress off, and this after nearly doing the same to her face. It had been a mortifying debacle of the highest order. Lila had never seen anything like it before, nothing close to the cowardice displayed by her date, her "newfound love," nothing close to the shrieking harridan he'd married and betrayed, nothing close to what the woman had done to her dress. She'd thought clothes ripped like that only in the movies. At a hundred and fifty dollars, she'd expected more integrity in the seams.

She hadn't vilified Robert; she'd left that for his wife to do. But neither had she forgiven herself for being fooled. She was smart, one of the smartest people she knew, and she hadn't seen through a two-timer. Loneliness and longing had clouded her judgment.

She was still lonely, and she still longed for the emotional and physical intimacy she'd had with her husband. But she no longer trusted herself in matters of the heart. It had been so easy with Danny, so very easy. There had been no other loves, no lies, no complications, no pasts. Nowadays, it seemed everyone she met had a past. She did, too, as of last year, and only by the grace of a miracle had that messy past left her still holding her job.

Robert had not only failed to mention he had a wife, he'd failed to mention his wife was the daughter of a congressman. A very messy business that, Lila had discovered, acquiring the enmity of a congressman's daughter. In the same way the congressman had gotten Robert on the team of the NASA project, he'd tried to get Lila out of her professorship. He'd almost succeeded, if only because the head of her department had his own political aspirations and feared the congressman would somehow hold him responsible for Lila's bad judgment. She'd held on to her job, but the head of her department had made it clear that tenure or not, as far as he was concerned she was on probation.

She wondered if Jack Hudson had any idea how risky love could be at their age. He must not, or he wouldn't be bandying the term around quite so freely. It wouldn't trip off his tongue with such lightness. She was mere months away from thirty, and he probably was a few years beyond her. Those first romances, the true loves filled with promise and purity, were behind them both. She didn't know if she could ever accept less, though.

Her gaze settled on the novel she'd brought in from the living room. Maybe her mother was right. Maybe it was time to put a little fantasy into her life. Reality, in the long, tall form of Jack Hudson, was getting too hot to handle.

The great thing about a shower, Jack thought, was the near impossibility of running out of cold water. Hot water was short-lived, fickle, unreliable, but good old cold water never let you down. It was always there, ready to freeze your body into immobility and your brain into a new set of desires, mostly to get warm again.

He opened his mouth under the stinging spray and shook his head, letting the shampoo lather sluice down his chest. Knowing he was in for a long night, he'd decided to start fresh with a head-clearing shower. Then he'd go to work and see if he could channel his sexual energies into something creative. Sexual energy ought to be good for something, he figured, especially since using it for actual sex didn't seem to be working out. Lila Singer would be the death of him, if pneumonia didn't get him first.

Half an hour later, blow-dried and bundled up, he stoked the potbellied stove in one corner of his custom-designed, three-bay, two-story garage. Rolling his oxyacetylene welding rig out across the concrete floor, he stopped beneath an expansive half arch of hard steel. He looked up at the structure through the web of surrounding scaffolding. Chains and pulleys held much of the sculpture in place, waiting for Jack's torch to meld the massive pieces into a whole, into art.

"Right, Jack. Art," he muttered, smiling wryly as he lowered his goggles and struck a spark. He didn't know about art, not the kind they taught at the university, but he knew when he got something right. He knew the emotional impact of line, the strength of material. He knew where to put space and where to put solid to build the vision in his head and heart.

He'd done metal sculpture since high school, but hadn't worked on a grand scale until after his divorce. He'd started for the sheer challenge of trying to balance the tremendous weight, make it do what he wanted. Over the course of the ensuing months, he'd discovered a personal harmony with the big pieces, a sense of power nothing under six feet in height had ever given him.

After melting his first rod, Jack walked over to a bank of stereo equipment protected inside a metal shelving unit. Speakers hung from six places high on the walls of the garage.

He pulled off one heavy leather glove with his teeth and pressed a series of soft-touch pads. Within seconds the aria from *Madama Butterfly* "Un bel di" filled the large building. He usually wasn't so emotionally sentimental, but then, he usually wasn't in love.

Lila reached for the book and settled herself back against a pile of pillows. The cover held her attention even longer than the first time she'd seen it. The Hawk did bear a striking resemblance to Jack. They both had the kind of average looks that were somehow made extraordinarily appealing by the personality behind them. They both had sandy brown hair and a lean muscularity. She scrutinized the cover more closely and began to wonder if Jack had the same enticing pattern of chest hair narrowing to a sleek band down the middle of his abdomen. She wondered about it for nearly five minutes before she snapped out of her daydreams and turned to the first page.

Fifteen minutes later she knew she was in for the long haul, and forced herself to put the book down so she could make a snack run. Fortified with cookies and a big glass of milk, she arranged herself back into the cozy warmth of her bed. Poor Jack, she thought, all alone in his bed without a good book to keep him company.

Poor Jack . . . she thought again, a little more slowly, with a little more feeling. *All alone in his bed.* She raised a cookie to her mouth and nibbled off an edge. She wondered if he was sleeping. He might be watching television, or a movie, or doing anything.

He suddenly seemed very far away. Every time he left, she missed him more than the time before. She didn't know what his home looked like, or if he'd even gone there after leaving her. She had his phone number, but calling him was out of the question. She couldn't remember ever having called a man for purely personal reasons, simply because she missed him, except for Danny, of course.

What if she called and he wasn't home? She'd only feel worse, which was a terrible thing to have to admit to herself. Jack Hudson was taking up far too much of her thinking, and he was turning it all upside down.

Calling him was out of the question.

Jack pushed his goggles to the top of his head and used his sleeve to wipe the sweat off his brow. A cup of coffee rested near his elbow, precariously balanced on a slight wedge of steel twelve feet above the floor. He took a sip.

It had been a good idea to spend the night in the garage working, figuring, meeting the challenge of getting a lot of big pieces of metal to look like one piece. He'd almost forgotten about Lila once or twice, especially since he'd changed the music to hard-driving rock and roll. He'd used the energy of the music to pull him through the more technically difficult welds, but he'd had enough energy and needed to listen to something of substance, something he could think about instead of just feel.

Of course, there was danger in thinking, because he inevitably ended up thinking of her. Was he really in love? he wondered. Or were his hormones doing a number on his brain?

Nice try, Jack, he thought, quietly laughing at himself. Nice try, but it's love, you fool.

He finished his coffee in one swallow and lowered his goggles back over his eyes. After a moment of summing up his next move, he struck a spark and flamed his torch.

Lila hung up the phone by her bed for the third time and calmly told herself she wasn't upset. It was none of her business what he did when he wasn't with her. It was none of her business what he was doing at ten-thirty on a Saturday night. It was none of her business whom he was talking to, smiling at, laughing with. None of her business at all.

She fluffed up her pillow behind her back and buried her nose in *Night of the Hawk*, where no matter how dangerous the situation or troubled the relationship, love always conquered doubts. The book was sexy too. Probably too sexy for her state of mind.

She hoped Jack wasn't smiling at another woman. His smiles were lethal, charmed, unsafe at any speed when it came to the female heart.

She flipped back a couple of pages, realizing she'd been thinking of Jack again instead of reading. She hoped he was having the same problem getting her out of his mind. She hoped he remembered their last kiss with the same unnerving clarity she did. She hoped she was driving him crazy.

By midnight she knew who was driving whom

crazy, but she decided to avoid the fact by going to sleep. When she woke up at two o'clock, she chastised herself for senseless infatuation and rolled over. At four o'clock, she admitted to having a real problem and maybe something more than infatuation. At six o'clock she got up and fixed a big pot of coffee, and every time she paced by her telephone bulletin board, she looked at his business card and the address printed across the bottom.

Eight

The sunrise spread a tapestry of orange-pinks and robin's-egg blue across the eastern sky and cast a blanket of frozen crystal diamonds across the snow-covered landscape. Lila slowed to a near stop on the icy country road and checked the business card and her county map again.

Sure, she felt foolish, driving out to his house at dawn on a Sunday morning, but between six and six-thirty that morning she'd worked herself up into a real case of the worries, especially when he hadn't answered his phone for the fourth time. The man had said he was falling in love with her. He'd said, "Call me." He hadn't mentioned anything about disappearing off the face of the earth.

Slick roads, a moonless night, below-freezing temperatures . . . She'd thought of them all. Anything could have happened to him, the same way something had happened to Danny. She wanted to check on him, make sure he was in one piece. Then she'd return home and go back to bed.

A windbreak of pines pinpointed a house on a ridge, and she knew it had to be his. There was nothing else for miles around. As she drove closer, any doubts she might have had dissipated. A large deck on the western side of the house was unfinished, and the front of the house looked as if it had been under construction for years. The carpenter who had built most of her office inside of a week didn't have time to finish his own porch.

The long, straight driveway led from the county road to a graveled area between the side of the house and the garage. And that garage was bigger than any Lila had seen before. It had a wide door twice the height of the average garage door. More unusual yet, the two windows cut into either side of a person-sized entrance glowed and flashed with a strange light.

She stopped her car and sat staring at the showers of sparks interspersed with darkness. What in the world?

His truck was parked next to the house, alleviating her initial fears, but those fears had been replaced by a curiosity powerful enough to change her original plans. Not that she needed much nudging to grab any handy excuse for seeing him. She wished she did. She felt slightly brazen, showing up uninvited to check on a man who had lived his whole life so far without any help or interference from her.

But he'd said he was falling in love, and the words had kept her awake most of the night. She was curious about the strange light coming from his garage, yes, but not nearly as curious as she was about how he'd come to be falling in love.

Truth be told, she had a sneaky suspicion the same thing might be happening to her, and she didn't have a clue as to how it might have begun or how it might end.

What drew two people together? Unexpected kisses on moonlit autumn nights? Unexpected kisses in half-finished office additions? Or was it the total polarization of education, experience, goals, and interests?

Nothing made sense. He had her breaking rules faster than she could remember them: dating him, kissing him, calling him, practically following him home.

Her car door creaked with the cold as she pushed it open, then she stepped onto the gravel drive. A gust of wind caught at her hair, blowing dark curls into her face. She brushed them back with a gloved hand and slammed the door shut.

Furthermore, she added silently, he had her doing things she'd never even thought to make rules against—like knocking on frozen wooden doors to metal garages at dawn. She didn't get an answer, and after another moment in the frigid air, she twisted the knob and pushed.

She immediately understood why he hadn't answered. The building was alive with music. Wagner's Valkyries thundered to the rafters and beyond on their way to Valhalla with their fallen warriors. It was heroic music to match the heroic sculpture half assembled and rising high from the middle of the garage floor.

The size and power inherent in the sweeping steel arches drew her gaze ever higher and caught the breath in her throat. Stunned, she took a step forward, but when sparks showered down from above, she hurriedly took a step backward. Keeping her eyes averted from the welding flame, she closed the door behind her and walked over to a table where she'd spotted an extra pair of goggles.

He was high on the scaffolding, balanced in the web of supporting steel rods with a safety harness around his waist. His torch burned and flamed along a juncture of two of the steel pieces. She didn't have any trouble recognizing him, not even in a backward baseball cap, goggles, and less-than-form-fitting denim coveralls. She'd spent enough of the last few weeks watching him work to know the unique authority he had in his hands, to know his special sureness of movement.

It was Jack all right, and he was sculpting steel with a welding torch, melting some pieces together, cutting through others, and turning the whole majestic melange into a soaring vision of strength, into a physical expression of emotion. The man who could do that with his hands didn't need to read books.

She walked around the scaffolding in a daze, careful to stay away from the sparks falling from above, but touching the metal where she could. The sculpture invited touch, from where it rose from its molten lavalike beginnings to the spiraling arches and half arches reaching toward the dawn-lightened sky she glimpsed through a skylight.

She traced a weld with her fingertip, following the scorched seam into a sweeping curve and up the next arc. Her hand looked small and fragile against the blue-black luster of the steel. The metal was cold, but the sculpture itself was hot, sizzling with power, electrified in its simplicity and grace. She had no trouble comprehending his intentions when she tilted her head back to take in the whole glorious thing. An abstract phoenix rose from the ashes, renewal pulsing in the heavy mesh and tracery of metal. He was an artist, and the tools he used demanded strength of conviction. There was no turning your back on a ton of precariously balanced steel.

There was no turning her back on him. What she felt standing there in the web of shadows of his creation wasn't something she could deny. The man who'd hidden none of his faults had suddenly revealed his innermost heart, and she saw the complexity she'd only sensed the day he'd seen Danny's photograph of her. She saw the intensity of personality she'd felt each time he'd kissed her. She now knew where his overwhelming passion came from—it was inherent in the man, and it wasn't purely sexual. He lived with passion inside him. He tempered it within the physical and structural constraints of building homes and gazebos that were sound and safe. Then he let it unfurl and fly when he sculpted and when he kissed, defying the laws of gravity with one and the laws of decorum with the other.

The sparks had stopped falling from above, and Lila realized the music had ended as well. She slowly lifted her gaze to meet his.

"Hi." His voice washed over her, deep and steady.

"Hi."

He hung in the air, bracketed by the scaffolding, the goggles pushed up on top of his cap. A smile teased the corners of his mouth, curious light gleamed in his eyes.

"Hungry?" he asked, his grin broadening a mile wide.

"Sure," she said softly. He made breaking all the rules so easy.

With a satisfied nod, he released himself from the harness and climbed down to the floor. She watched as he shut off his equipment and shrugged out of the coverall. She had a million questions, but asked none of them. An acute attack of shyness had stolen her tongue. She wouldn't have left for anything, but it didn't make staying any less difficult. His assumption about why she'd showed up at his house at sunrise was probably correct, and he knew it involved more than just breakfast.

Jack was nervous, too, and higher than a kite that she'd come. As far as he was concerned, the morning couldn't last long enough. He remembered the expression on her face in the photograph, and he wanted it for himself, for what there could be between him and the dark-eyed woman who haunted his dreams.

She'd come to him. He turned and extended his hand, his smile a permanent fixture. After a short hesitation, she gave him her hand.

He noticed the slight quaver of her mouth and her averted gaze. She looked ready to bolt. She also looked incredibly lovely. The cold had pinkened her cheeks and the tip of her nose. The wind had blown her hair into a riotous tumble of curls. The upturned collar of her mink coat framed her face, and the lush fur and silken strands of her hair contrasted sensually with the cool creaminess of her skin. She looked ready to be touched. Her mouth, full and sweet, looked ready to be kissed. But he didn't want to make any mistakes.

He entwined his fingers with hers, taking his time and encouraging the small smile trying to form on her face. When she glanced up, he lifted their hands to his mouth and brushed his lips across her knuckles.

"You picked a good time to come. Breakfast is my favorite meal. I always go all-out."

Her smile came, brief and sweet, and shy enough to increase his confidence. "I thought you looked like a good breakfast man."

"I could be your good anytime man," he said, soft and low, and watched an instant flush of embarrassment spread across her face. She lowered her gaze again, and in repentance he bent down and whispered in her ear, "How do you like your eggs?"

"Scrambled." *Like my emotions,* she added silently, *and my nerves, and my senses when you're this close.*

"Scrambled it is," he said, tucking her against his side and directing her out the door.

Her few minutes in the relative warmth of the garage made the outside air feel cold to the point of breathlessness. Or was that him stealing her breath?

Their boots crunched across the wide gravel driveway, squeaking against the frozen rocks. She began shivering. He pulled her tighter and lengthened his stride until she had to run to keep up.

"Almost there," he said.

"G-good," she chattered back, and hoped it really was the cold and not her nerves making her tremble from the inside out.

When they reached the house, he swung her onto the front porch, past the half-finished parts, then jumped up beside her. Two more steps brought them to the large, carved wood door. She barely had time to register the intricate landscape cut into the heavy oak before he whisked her inside.

"I'll have you warmed up in no time," he assured her.

That was exactly what she was afraid of.

His house was a mess, but not in the usual sort of ways. He'd invited her to take a tour while he fixed breakfast, and she'd taken him up on his offer, with some wildly unexpected results. She was lost, and she was jealous. The first she knew she could remedy by backtracking. The second so flabbergasted her, she wasn't sure what to think. But every time she turned back to the bathtub sunk into the terra-cotta floor and saw the voluptuous bronze mermaid wrapped around its curving sides, Lila's mouth tightened a bit more. The mermaid's smile was very personal, and the name Christina had been worked into the tiny scales, along with a date two years old. Jack was obviously a man of many talents. She'd never seen a sculpture so drenched in sensuality. The tail fanned out along the back of the bathtub, making what looked like a perfect place to rest a person's head while they relaxed in the hot water. The mermaid held bluish copper conch shells in her hands, which was where the water poured forth.

No shells covered her breasts, but the wall behind the sink was inset with real seashells, hundreds of them, in all shapes and sizes, framing the mirror with no discernible pattern. The wildness of the display, coupled with a free-standing metallic garden of seaweed, and aqua-tinted blown glass in the window casing, gave the room a definite watery atmosphere.

Lila stepped back out into the hall and ducked under a two-by-four propped against the wall. She knew the living room, with its panoramic view of the unfinished western deck, was somewhere behind her, past the "undersea" bathroom, a surprisingly stark room with a drafting table in it, and a kitchen where no one had skimped on the windows or the exotic tile work. She chose the uncharted territory ahead and found herself stepping over gallons of paint and tubs of plaster, until she reached the sanctuary of his bedroom.

Serenity reigned over the mellow oak floors covered with hand-braided rugs in shades of blue and white. Three of the walls were plastered. The remaining wall was paneled in whitewashed one-by-fours. Four lightly stained totem poles held up his bed.

Lila walked farther into the room. She touched the multicolored quilt spread between the totem poles and ran a fingertip over a row of hand stitching. Her gaze took in the simple furnishings: a wooden dresser against one wall, two pine bedside tables. His house was the strangest she'd ever seen, beautiful but strange. Half the rooms were chaos incarnate, like the "undersea" bathroom with its mermaid and the kitchen with its wild tile on the counters, floors, and walls; and half the rooms were functional yet warm, unadorned yet elegant. It was as if two different people lived in the house, two people incapable of compromise.

Of course, she thought with a sudden flash of memory, he was divorced. There had been two people in the house, Jack and Christina, she of the bare breasts and lovely smile.

With a sigh, Lila backed away from the bed. She had no business being there. Christmas vacation was obviously proving to be too much of a strain on her. She needed classes, lectures to prepare and give, the immediacy of exams. Hanging around had gotten her into trouble last year, and this year was proving to be no different. She could see the essay assignment now—What I Did on My Christmas Vacation—and her answer in one page or less. "I talked myself into falling for the carpenter who was building a room onto my house. He turned out to have a lot of talents, not the least of which was his way with a kiss." No matter how she curved the grading scale, she had to give herself an F for failure to learn from previous lessons.

There was no such thing as true love anymore, she believed, not at her age and not in the society she lived in. Once was more than most people got, and she'd had her once with Danny.

The sudden finality of her reasoning took the wind out of her sails, and a small, traitorous part of her heart wished she could have had her once with Jack Hudson instead.

She lifted a hand to her breast and inhaled sharply, the sheer sacrilege of her last thought startling her pulse into a jump. She definitely needed to get back to work, the sooner the better. Even this morning couldn't be too quick. There was always something to do in her office at the university. Maybe Didi would be in, and they could talk about literature and things. Things like Jack Hudson.

"Lila?"

She whirled around as she heard him call her name. At the next moment he was there, standing in the doorway of his bedroom, and she knew she wasn't going anywhere. For reasons she didn't want to analyze any longer and couldn't explain, she needed him. She needed the warmth of his smile and the strength of his arms. She needed his easy laughter and his sure hands. She needed the thrill of his kisses, and she only prayed she was right to need anything at all from him.

"Breakfast is ready," he said, offering her his hand.

She liked holding his hand. She liked that he wanted to touch her, to keep her close.

"Sorry about the construction," he continued, helping her over the tubs of plaster and paint, "but I never seem to find time to work on my own house."

"I know what you mean," she said, following him down the hall. "I started to write a book once, but I found out I'm a lot better at critiquing other people's books."

"I guess that's the same thing." When they cleared the hallway, he pulled her under his arm, and she automatically slipped her hand around his waist.

"I noticed the one bathroom looks finished," she said. The words popped out, unbidden, unwelcome. Sabotage, she thought with an internal groan. Somewhere inside her was a subconscious necessity to sabotage any possible relationship with Jack Hudson.

"Actually," he said, "both bathrooms are finished. There's one in the master bedroom. After Christina, my ex-wife, put the seashells and seaweed in the main bath, I needed someplace else to brush my teeth. I got too dizzy in there." He laughed.

So she'd been right about his wife, Lila thought. That was a hollow victory at best. "She did the work herself?"

"Christina has taken the pursuit of arts and crafts to new heights and some new lows, if not quite to art itself." A bare, almost indiscernible sarcasm colored his words, and Lila looked up at him in surprise. She hadn't thought him capable of a discouraging word, let alone sarcasm. "She did the tile work in the kitchen," he added. "She ordered the front door as well, and it was all I could do to keep her from roofing the house in a checkerboard pattern of purple, green, and yellow."

"Sounds like a free spirit."

"She was free with a lot of things she shouldn't have been." With that intriguing statement, they reached the kitchen and he changed the subject. "I made eggs Benedict, but I scrambled yours instead of poaching them."

"Thanks," she murmured. "It looks wonderful." And it did. He'd set them up in the breakfast nook, by the bay window that looked out on the mountains to the west. Mugs of coffee steamed next to plates of hash browns, fresh fruit, and twin mounds of eggs Benedict floating in pools of hollandaise sauce.

She hesitated for a moment before sitting down, feeling compelled to add an apology for dropping in on him unannounced and receiving such royal treatment. No matter what words she came up with, though, they seemed inappropriate, even ridiculous. He'd said he was falling in love, and he hadn't questioned her arrival with so much as a lifted eyebrow. He'd accepted her presence as part of the natural order of life. He'd opened his home as if she belonged. He'd cooked her an incredible breakfast. Cooked, not zapped in a microwave or popped out of a toaster. She was impressed and a little self-conscious. She'd never made eggs Benedict in her life, and he'd whipped a whole meal up in less than half an hour. For a man who believed in the importance of women's traditional roles, he'd picked a poor example of womankind to be entertaining at his breakfast table.

Of course, he didn't know she couldn't cook. For all of her other gaffes, Lila figured she'd keep that particular fact to herself for a while—just in case he really was falling in love.

Nine

Jack smiled wryly to himself as Lila sat down, her gaze focused on her plate. If she weren't so skittish, he'd share the reason for the grin he couldn't seem to get off his face.

With typical brilliance, he'd gotten everything backward. Most people made love, slept, then ate breakfast. Not him though. Smooth Jack got right down to the salient point, the cardinal reason, the sum and substance for entertaining a beautiful woman—sharing breakfast. He'd inconveniently skipped all the fun parts.

All the really fun parts, he amended, like unbuttoning her shirt, starting with the pearly one at the very top, the one almost hidden by her lace collar. He'd never forgive himself for that oversight. Or sliding his hand over her breast. He'd been a fool to forget that part. No other man on the face of the earth would have forgotten to kiss her breathless before breakfast. The more he thought about it, the more he was beginning to hate himself and his dyslexic ways. He should have at least kissed her. Any other man would have kissed her before breakfast.

A quick check of her plate proved it wasn't too late.

The scraping of his chair was the only warning Lila got of the meltdown headed her way. She glanced up, and the impact of Jack's steady gaze and the realization of his intent shot through her like the finest, headiest wine. In seconds, his mouth was upon hers, warm, insistent, demanding, and sweeter than any memories she could conjure up. His tongue stroked down the length of hers with drugging sensuality, blowing fuses in her nerve endings. Her fork clattered to her plate. He slipped his hands under her arms, pulling her out of the chair. Her napkin slid to the floor, and only the strength of his embrace kept her from doing the same.

From somewhere in the house she heard the muted strains of a golden oldie tune, something about "Rescue me," and she prayed no one would bother. She didn't need rescuing. She needed Jack, and she showed him the depth of her need in a hundred different ways—with the subtle pressure of her body against his, with the slow caress of her hands through his hair, with the soft sounds and softer sighs he elicited with his touch.

Every stroke of his hands left a shimmering trail of sensation across her skin and deeper, where her emotions were unraveling with unheard-of speed. He was kissing her crazy, stealing her breath and whatever sense she might have brought with her. She didn't care, not even when she felt him tug her shirt out of the back of her pants, not even when his hand slid up her back and she felt the snap give way on her bra.

All she cared about was him pulling her toward him, slanting his mouth across hers to deepen the kiss. She cared about the heaviness of his breathing and how she wanted more. She cared about the heat of his skin and the taste of his mouth. She cared about making love now and making the loving last forever . . . forever and ever with Jack Hudson. The hardness of him, his strength and gentleness, the erotic power he wielded with his kiss, intoxicated her.

He should have known it would happen like this, Jack thought, fast and unstoppable. Breakfast had been consigned to ancient history. The only reality was the woman in his arms, Lila, she of the dark eyes and honeyed mouth. She of the sultry curves, the full breasts, the sleek hips.

He slid his hands to the front of her pants, released the snap, and undid the zipper. He wanted to slip his hands inside, but he was no fool. He knew there were limits, and he wanted to play them right to the edge. He wanted to savor and love her. He wanted to take her clothes off and start at her toes and not stop until her mouth melted under his again. He wanted her to explore him.

He wasn't letting her go this time. The phone was unplugged. The doors were locked, and neither his sister nor his father had a key. If he'd had time, he would have gone down to the county road and hung a Do Not Disturb sign on his mailbox. She was his. The magic of a long-ago night was coming to life in his arms.

He'd been right to kiss her under the harvest

moon. The promise he'd felt hadn't been forsaken by the months of waiting. In truth, nothing could have been sweeter or hotter than the fire she was lighting from one end of his senses to the other. She touched him, and he wanted more. She kissed him, and he felt the wild abandon of her heart match his.

She needed his loving. She pressed against him, her hands pulling his shirt from his pants, her mouth alternately teasing and aggressive. Jack knew the smartest thing he'd ever done in his whole life was to kiss her before breakfast.

He felt cotton slide from beneath denim, then her hands were on him, warm and small, flattening against the tense plane of his abdomen and making it even tenser. His breathing stopped of its own accord. His hand stilled on the nape of her neck.

With the gentlest care he rubbed his mouth over hers, dragging a deep breath into his lungs. Her response was immediate and surprising. Her fingers slowly curled around his waistband, and one by one she undid the buttons on his jeans.

"Ah, Lila," he murmured, feeling a rush of arousal spread through his body.

They left a trail of clothes from the kitchen to his bedroom. Jack shrugged out of his shirt and spent thirty seconds fighting with the cuff button on his left wrist before he broke it off and wadded the shirt into a pile, which he inadvertently dropped into the hollandaise bowl in the sink.

Lila slipped out of her shirt like cream pouring from a pitcher, smoothly, with flowing grace. The midnight-blue silk blouse floated toward the floor catching on a cupboard handle and hanging there like a testimonial flag to love. He kissed her exposed shoulder, his mouth running in a hot trail down the side of her neck, his hands pushing the tiny white straps of her bra off her arms. The delicate piece of lingerie ended up draped across the fruit bowl.

Jack kicked off his tennis shoes in the hall. Lila stepped out of her flats in front of the "undersea" bathroom. They paused beneath the two-by-four, where Jack taught her the delights of a bare bosom pressed against a hardened, muscled chest covered with silky dark hair. It was a lesson she never wanted to end, not when he simultaneously whispered erotic promises in her ear.

His previous kisses should have been fair warning of the fire he was igniting all along her body. His sculpture should have prepared her for the imagination inherent in his words. But five years of marriage and one three-week debacle of a love affair had obviously left some blanks in her sexual experiences.

"No," she exclaimed softly, her face flaming even as her own imagination embellished his sensual murmurings.

He grinned and gently bit her neck. "Yes."

She tilted her head back, another denial on her lips, but what she saw in his eyes left it unspoken. The man loved her. He wanted to give her everything, and she had a sneaky suspicion he could—like nothing and nobody she'd ever dreamed up.

"Jack, I . . ." Her voice trailed off in uncertainty. She wanted to tell him something, say something to explain how she felt about him, but she couldn't find the right words. "I'm—I'm glad I came this morning."

"Good." His mouth brushed across her brow as his hand caressed upward toward her breast.

"But . . ."

"Shh." He filled his palm with her, and she felt his sigh against her skin.

"There was someone else." The words came hesitantly, and she wondered if that was what she'd meant to say all along. Somehow she didn't think so.

"You don't have to tell me." He stepped backward, continuing down the hall toward his bedroom, pulling her with him, kissing her cheek, her temple, the side of her nose.

"It wasn't very good," she added haltingly. "Or admirable. It was pretty terrible."

"I'll make it better." He tunneled his hand through her hair and lifted it away from her neck. His mouth traced a path along her nape, his tongue searing her skin.

Breathless, her heart pounding, Lila let him lead her into his bedroom. A part of her mind kept wondering where all the extraneous doubts were hiding and when they would jump out and fill her with guilt, embarrassment, reticence. Her confession certainly hadn't done it, but something had to happen to ruin these marvelous feelings. Some internal switch must have been delayed.

Or Jack had derailed it, she thought, because no anxiety surfaced when he backed her up to his bed and pushed her slacks over her hips. Only excitement happened—deep down, thrilling, sensual excitement laced with a heady dose of anticipation. His hands, so strong and sure, were on her, all over her, guiding and pleasing, and undressing her with a confidence she responded to without hesitation.

Her limbs were heavy with the need to hold him closer. Her mouth searched for his as he followed her down to the bed, leaving his jeans in a pile on the floor next to hers.

"I'm in love with you," he said between soft, slow kisses. He cupped her face in his hands, his thumbs tracing her cheekbones, his warm masculine body pressed against the length of hers. "I wanted you to know that."

"Thank you." She sighed the words and heard his deep chuckle echo against her skin.

"You're welcome." He kissed her once more, then lifted his head. A lazy smile graced his mouth. A slumberous passion darkened his eyes. "You're very pretty"—his gaze drifted down in perfect tandem with his hand—"everywhere."

"Thank you," she said again in a hushed whisper, all of her senses intent on the path he was taking.

"You're welcome," he drawled, and she felt the smile in his words. He stopped at her knee, then lightly stroked up the silky length of her inner thigh. Her eyes fluttered closed as she moaned. How did he make her melt with each touch? she wondered. What instinct gave him the magic to thrill her with such sensitivity?

What manner of man had she fallen in love with? And where were all her inhibitions?

Fallen in love with?

"Jack?"

"Hmm?"

"Something is happening."

"No kidding." He slid his leg between hers and

lowered his mouth to her breast. After several tantalizing moments, he moved to her other breast, and Lila felt his low groan ricochet through her chest. He was devouring her sweetly, completely, his mouth roaming at will over her body, teasing her, tasting her, fulfilling the promise of his whispered words.

She sank deeper under his spell with every second of pleasure, until the pleasure grew too intense and her need for more of him grew undeniable.

With a slight shift of her body and the guiding tenderness of her hands, she silently asked him to return to her mouth for her kiss. When he did, the magic started all over, heightened by the pressure of his arousal between her thighs. He slipped partway inside, deepening the kiss to match. Slowly, degree by breathtaking degree, he made her completely his own.

She didn't remember love ever being so intensely sweet, with each movement lifting them to a higher level of sensation and her feeling so safe in abandoning herself to the moment and the man who held her. She placed wild kisses on his face and throat and mouth, always his mouth, his divinely designed mouth so adept at drenching her senses in passion.

Jack matched her kiss for kiss, until he felt time running out. He wanted to be inside her forever, playing on the edge of maximum excitement and total satiation, but she had a way about her, a way of tightening around him with each thrust, a way of sighing in his ear and driving him over that sweet, delicate edge. All of his energy coalesced into one urgent desire—to take her, and take her quickly, to the place where she was taking him.

He plunged deeply and stopped long enough to capture her gasp with his mouth. Then he moved again, and again, quickening his tempo in response to the thousand subtle signals her body sent to his.

When the end came, he found his eternity in her sweet contractions around him, in the whisper of his name on her lips, in the tightness of her embrace.

Cocooned in contentment, Lila nuzzled her face into the broad shoulder supporting her head. Every atom of her being felt worked over, supremely used and renewed. Her skin still tingled, nerve impulses still imploded softly along the length of her body. She'd never known love could feel the way it felt with Jack. She'd loved Danny, but there had always been something elusive about him even in making love, something distracted and dreamy. He'd been hard to hold on to, and ultimately, she'd lost him.

But Jack, for all the sensitivity of his artistic soul, was there with her one hundred percent. She'd never been the recipient of so much concentrated attention, and she liked it—a lot. Even after only one dose, she suspected she might be addicted.

She turned her face up to his and kissed his jaw, eliciting a heavy sigh from deep in his chest. He rolled on top of her, his eyes still closed, and began to love her all over again.

• • •

"We can't go on like this," she murmured, snuggling closer to his warmth, her legs tangled with his.

"Speak for yourself," he muttered in her ear before proceeding with the path he was gently gnawing down her shoulder to her breast.

"I'm hungry," she said, her sigh quickly turning into a catch in her throat.

Jack was torn. He had food, lots of food, but he also had her in his arms, and she was starting to do all those little things she'd been doing all morning to tell him she was ready to make love again. He'd never known a woman to be so innately responsive. She did things, wild things, to his ego and his desire that both surprised and fascinated him. The softness in her eyes pulled on him; the other-worldly rapture she bestowed on him bewitched him. She'd blossomed under his caress, giving him more than he'd seen in the photograph, and she was ready to give to him again, as he was ready to give to her.

But she was hungry.

With a groan, he levered himself up on one elbow and reached over to the nightstand closest to him patting around in the drawer until he found what he wanted.

Lila laughed when she saw what he offered. "You keep a box of cookies in your bedroom?"

"For emergencies," he said, kissing her cheek before opening the gold box and checking the contents. "This is the variety pack. Chocolate covered mint, chocolate fudge without mint, chocolate-chocolate chip, regular chocolate chip with pecans, and chocolate—peanut butter swirls."

"Doesn't sound like much of a variety."

"I'm a consistent kind of guy."

"Justine's?" she guessed correctly.

"I harbor an undying love for the woman and her cookie sheets."

"And her cake pans," Lila added, teasing him.

"And her cake pans," he agreed, grinning. "So what's it going to be? Fudge, chips, nuts, mint, peanut butter . . . or me?" His eyes met hers, his smile slowly faded, and his last words came out so wistfully she couldn't resist.

Minutes later she was wonderfully glad she hadn't resisted. Loving Jack was sheer decadence, an indulgence of the senses. Maybe she had been alone too long. Or maybe the man in her arms was everything her heart had been telling her he was, while her mind had been searching for problems and running from the possibility of love.

When he touched her, she came alive. When he gave himself to her, she felt fulfilled. What he took in return, she didn't miss. Hope grew where only denial had been before. Maybe it was time to trust herself again. She certainly trusted Jack.

"Fudge, please."

"We're out of fudge. How about a chocolate—peanut butter swirl?"

Lila rolled over onto her side to face him, staring at him in disbelief. "You ate the last fudge cookie?"

"No, darlin'," he drawled. "You did."

"Oh."

"Oh," he repeated, not bothering to hide his grin. "Are you having fun yet?"

She nodded with only the barest hint of a blush. She couldn't have imagined more fun if she'd had a year to think it all up. Making love with Jack and sharing a whole box of Justine's cookies in bed had hit the top of her all-time-most-fun list. He made everything natural, carefree. His lack of self-consciousness was catching. He loved her.

Could it really be that easy? she asked herself. To make love and find love in a morning? The nice, thick barrier of skepticism she'd been carrying around for a year had melted under his touch, leaving her wondering. But even the serious nature of her musings didn't dim her fancy for another cookie. She peeked into the box resting on his abdomen.

"You can tell me about him now," he said, "if you want."

She paused with her fingers hovering over the last chocolate-chocolate chip. "Who?"

"You didn't mention him by name, but you said something about pretty terrible and not very good or admirable."

"Oh . . . him." She withdrew her hand and made a move to put some distance between her and Jack.

He stopped her by gently grasping her wrist. "I can wait until you're ready."

She glanced up. "I'm not sure why I spoke of him at all."

"Did he hurt you?"

She shook her head. "He shocked me, humiliated me, and in the end disgusted me, but no, he didn't hurt me." She paused for a moment, then whispered the truth. "He hurt his wife."

Jack quietly absorbed the information, watching her and feeling the sense of betrayal in her words.

"I—I didn't know," she said softly. "It was a real mess. We were at the Washington Center last Christmas. She came looking for him, found us instead, and went berserk. I never blamed her, except for ripping my dress and almost costing me my job. The whole sordid affair lasted less than three weeks and left me feeling horrible until . . ." Her eyes slowly met his. ". . . until this morning. Jack, I—"

Gazing at him, feeling the warmth of his arm around her, she wanted to tell him what she'd learned while making love. She wanted to tell him she loved him. But she'd used those words once by mistake, and had thereby cheapened them. She'd had some cockamamie idea that those three words would salve her conscience. She'd thought saying I love you would vanquish all the doubts she'd felt about going to bed with Robert. In short, she'd been a fool.

Now she looked at herself, lounging in bed with a man she'd been making love with all morning, not a shred of guilt in sight, and no false claims of love. Maybe she shouldn't rock the boat.

Jack kept himself from pushing her to finish her thoughts out loud, sensing her need for caution. He knew what they had between them. He was willing to wait for her to come to her own realizations in her own time. He had what he wanted. She was with him, and he wasn't letting her go.

"It won't happen again, Lila," he said, turning her into his arms and cradling her love-warmed, naked body against his. He brushed a kiss across her brow. When she lifted her face, he covered her mouth with his own, more than willing to love her yet again, to love any remnants of her doubts and pain away.

Starvation woke her, manifested as a great rumbling sound from the vicinity of her stomach. Woman, she decided, could not live on love and cookies forever. She needed sustenance, while Jack, it seemed, needed sleep.

Late afternoon sunshine bathed him in a golden glow, burnishing his skin to a soft copper against the pure whiteness of the sheets. He stretched the length of the bed, six feet of delectable maleness. An unsolicited sigh escaped her lips, and she had to remind herself what she was about.

Her gaze drifted over his still form once more, taking in the sun-weathered lines feathering from the corners of his eyes, the sweep of brown hair brushed away from his forehead, the curve of the muscles in his arm, and she knew he was the man she loved. When he awakened, she vowed to tell him.

She slipped from his side, making sure the quilt covered him and resisting the urge to tuck the blanket around him, to smooth his hair, maybe bestow a loving kiss on his cheek. He'd be there when she returned from the kitchen.

Her slacks were crumpled on the floor next to his jeans, but her blouse was nowhere to be found. She settled for a sweatshirt she saw lying on his dresser. The heavy black cotton shirt had big silver letters spread across the chest. RAIDERS. Lila grinned. He was a renegade all right. Few people in

Bronco territory had the guts to sport the logo of the Denver team's arch rival.

She found her shoes where she'd left them in front of the aquatic bathroom. As she continued down the hall, she expected at any moment to see her bra and blouse. But she made it to the kitchen without finding them, and once she got there, she forgot all about her clothes.

She stopped stock still in the doorway, her eyes wide with mortification, and let the world crash down around her for a good fifteen seconds before she whirled around and raced away. She grabbed her coat and purse by the front door. She stumbled across the porch and jumped down to the ground. Her car earned her everlasting gratitude by starting on the first try, and she tore down the driveway, leaving a plume of frozen snow in her wake.

When she hit the county road, she lurched to a stop and squeezed her eyes shut. She shouldn't have run away. It was childish, ridiculous, stupid—but she'd be damned if she was going back.

"Mermaids," she hissed, slamming her hand against the steering wheel.

The banging of the front door startled Jack awake. Who in the world? he wondered, pushing himself upright. His first intention was to assure Lila everything was okay. But one glance at the bed made it all too obvious what had happened.

He flopped back down on the pillows, biting out a sharp expletive. A moment later he threw one arm over his face, let out a deep sigh, and muttered the word again. If she wasn't the most confusing woman he'd ever met, she ran a damn close second.

Hadn't they just spent an incredible morning together? He'd certainly never had another one even remotely similar. He was about ready to nominate himself into the *Guinness Book of World Records*. Lord, but the lady did crazy things to him.

Hadn't he bided his time, been patient, wooed and courted her? Yes. But hadn't he also bulldozed her into his bed that morning? Maybe.

Yet hadn't she looked at him with those, you-could-drown-in-them brown eyes of hers and all but told him she loved him?

The last question hung in his mind for a long time, unanswered. He didn't know. He didn't know anything anymore. He didn't believe for a minute he was capable of falling in love all by himself, or that he could have misinterpreted everything they'd done and shared in the last few hours, let alone the last month.

So now what? he asked himself. Get up? Get dressed? Go after her? Or would that really make a fool of him?

Yes, the answer came to him. That would really make a fool of him. The lady had run out on him. He had to respect her decision, no matter how totally incomprehensible it was. Totally. Incomprehensible.

He swore again.

"Goodness, Jack. I haven't heard that kind of language out of you in years."

For a split second the feminine voice paralyzed him. Then he groaned and swore again, repeatedly, under his breath. He lowered his forearm an inch and peered over his wrist, and his swearing gained some volume.

She stood there, tall and willowy and built, silky blond hair flowing like a sheet of satin to her waist, her only makeup a California tan, her blue eyes wide and innocent. "I didn't mean to scare your paramour off, honest. I just dropped by to see you and do a few things, pick up a few things. I barely caught her out of the corner of my eye before she disappeared. The next thing I knew, the front door slammed. Didn't you tell her about me, Jack?"

She had Lila's bra and blouse in one hand, and Jack didn't trust himself to speak. Women were funny about things like that. Lila had probably hit the ceiling just before she'd hit the front door.

"Don't worry, Jack. I'm sure she'll be back. You were always the best catch around. She'll be back."

In silent fury he whipped the sheets back and got out of bed.

"You're looking good, Jack . . . real good."

He maintained his silence and his fury until he had his jeans on and buttoned. Then he turned to his ex-wife.

"Everybody looks good to you, Christina. That was one of our problems."

Ten

It had taken three days, but the shock was finally wearing off. She'd seen his wife, or rather his ex-wife, standing in his kitchen, holding up her, Lila's, silk and lace blouse and giving an odd look to the brassiere nestled over the grapes, apples, and oranges in the fruit bowl. She'd recognized the woman instantly from the sculpture in the bathroom, though when she'd seen the sculpture she hadn't believed anyone had hair that flowed to her waist in unbroken perfection, or that anyone so slender in the hips could be so abundantly endowed in the chest.

She couldn't believe he'd been married to a blond goddess, or that after having had such a woman he'd be content settling for a slighter model—a much slighter model. She couldn't believe she'd gotten herself in trouble over Christmas break again, and she couldn't believe where her bra had ended up.

She felt shameless.

Thank the Lord she still had her job and no explaining to do to anyone except herself. Fortunately, she was barely on speaking terms with herself, so no explanations had been required thus far.

Lila paused in her lecture for a second to gather her thoughts. She looked over the sea of expectant faces in the classroom, or maybe scattered ponds of expectant faces was a truer description. Typically, a fair portion of her students were busy doing something other than listening to her expound on *Wuthering Heights,* and a small but determined group were equally busy doing absolutely nothing, unless playing Lost in Space was the new rage on campus.

A hand went up in the front row, where most of the hand raising went on, and Lila nodded to the young woman.

"I don't see the connection between Greek mythology and *Wuthering Heights,*" the student began in an authoritative tone, "unless you've skipped ahead in the syllabus to the Bible portion of the semester and are trying to make a case for Heathcliff as a tortured Messiah figure, which, quite frankly, Dr. Singer, you're going to have a hard time doing."

Lila stared at the young woman in silence, noting her very pale makeup, her carmine red lipstick, and the seriously black dye job on her short cropped hair. The young woman was "in," an updated version of a beatnik, and she was right about Heathcliff.

"Of course," Lila agreed, sneaking a glance at her watch. The big hand was on the twelve and the little hand was on the eleven, exactly where they'd been when she'd gone for lunch quite a while ago. So what time was it now, she wondered, and what class was she supposed to be teaching?

"Greek mythology, of course," she reminded herself aloud, then quickly covered her mistake. "Greek mythology, of course, has no direct relation to the theme of *Wuthering Heights*, but an astute critical analysis of any piece of classical literature will turn up recurring threads of meaning referring to the human condition which have their base in ancient mythologies and religions."

"Of course," the young woman replied, as if she'd finally heard something worthwhile. "Is this what you'll be looking for on the essay portion of our exams?"

"Of course," Lila said, then on an uncharacteristic whim added, "Class dismissed."

Those who had been listening looked momentarily confused. Those who had been sleeping with their eyes open burst from the room with amazing speed.

Lila turned away from the podium and sank into one of the chairs lined up behind the table at the front of the classroom. *Wuthering Heights* in Greek mythology class? She was losing it. Worse, it had taken far too long for one of her budding intellectuals to catch her mistake. She had no idea what in the world the rest of them had been thinking. She did know, however, exactly what she'd been thinking, and it had had very little to do with either *Wuthering Heights* or Greek mythology.

She'd had a long day. Make that three long days and three very short nights. She rested her head in her hands, then slowly let it slide to the desk and the cradle of her arms.

She'd been run out of her own house. Jack still had his key and he'd been using it every evening, requiring her to spend a good portion of her nights imposing on her parents, or going to the library, or eating out by herself until the fast food joints shut down and he left her home for his.

She knew she'd made a complete and utter fool of herself. She just wasn't sure when. Had going to bed with him and having such a glorious morning been the foolish thing? Or had bolting out the door been her folly? A little of both, she'd decided, or, rather, a lot of both. At least she hadn't compounded her mistake by writing him another letter. Of course, silence could be considered pretty foolish too.

She heard someone enter the room, and she peeked up just enough to check her watch. It seemed early for the next class, but then, she couldn't tell by her watch, the darn thing. To save herself any possible embarrassment, she decided to go hide out in her office.

Muffling a sigh, she lifted her head and cast a casual, uninterested glance at the other person in the room. The look she got in return was anything but casual or uninterested. Hazel eyes swept over her with an intensity she remembered all too well, sending a thrill down to her toes and a flush across her cheeks.

She'd made love with him, this man with the sexily disheveled appearance of someone who might not be getting enough sleep either. His white shirt was rumpled and open at the collar, revealing a tender triangle of skin dusted with silky hair. She remembered the taste of him there. She remembered the warm, solid beat of his pulse beneath her lips, the life of him.

Her gaze drifted down to his sawdust- and plaster-dusted jeans. Was it her imagination, or were his jeans riding a little lower on his hips? Had he lost weight? She had, even with her lousy eating habits. Five pounds in three days. Four days, if she counted Sunday.

She looked back up at his face, knowing she should say something, but all she came up with were memories of the time she'd spent in his arms, tangled in his sheets and wrapped in the heat of his lovemaking.

She knew what fantasies lay behind the banked fire in his eyes, because he'd told her in whispers. He'd told her with his touch. She knew how it felt to be held by him in the most intimate embrace, how the muscles in his arms flexed, how the tautness of his abdomen felt against the softness of hers. She knew the sound of him in love. She knew the scent of him. The very essence of him was imprinted on her memory with indelible delicacy.

She wanted to cry.

Jack didn't feel like crying, but he saw on her face all the signs of an imminent flood of tears.

"I missed you after you left," he said, his voice husky and low. She blinked twice, and he immediately realized he'd said the wrong thing.

"Christina apologized for using her key unannounced," he said as a second attempt. It was a bit of a lie, but he was just a man trying to do his best. "I should have changed the locks years ago."

Missed again, he thought, watching a pink flush spread across her face like a mask.

"I guess school is keeping you pretty busy . . . even at night." Subtlety wasn't his strong point, but he was still trying.

She brushed her cheek, automatically extending the movement to tuck a straying curl behind her ear, then began organizing books, notes, and pencils. "No, not really," she said, forgetting to politely lie. "Not yet anyway. The semester isn't even a week old."

That was not what Jack had wanted to hear, not even close. She was telling him something, probably the same thing she'd tried to tell him by leaving on Sunday, and he was just being too damned stubborn to accept it.

To hell with subtlety, he decided.

"Why haven't you returned my phone calls?"

Before she had time to answer, a movement at the door caught his eye, and he silently cursed. His timing really needed work. Students were coming in for the next class, right in the middle of his big scene.

"I've been busy," she said in a shaky voice, not meeting his gaze and forgetting she'd forgotten to lie before. She rose from the chair, scraping the legs back with a disconcerting screech, and picked up her books.

"You just said you weren't." He strode over to her and took the books out of her arms. She let him have them despite a brief nervous glance. "Have you had lunch?"

She paused to let a student pass in front of her and absently checked her watch. She gave it a shake. "Yes. Hours ago."

"How about dinner?" Jack asked, weaving through the crowd to keep up with her.

"I . . . uh—"

"Hey, Dr. Singer!" an exuberant masculine voice interrupted. "You teaching this class?"

Jack eyed the much younger man elbowing his way to a very flustered Lila. Muscle beach, he thought. The kid was rippling with them, and most of them were exposed. His torn T-shirt didn't quite meet his jeans, which were so skin-tight Jack was sure he was going to hurt himself. He could only hope, considering the definitely appreciative gleam in the kid's sinfully blue eyes.

Jack would never have touted himself as an expert on women, but he knew enough about them to guess how most of them would react to the black-haired Italian stallion headed in Lila's direction. The kid looked like a hothouse model, with the kind of face that made young girls swoon and older women wonder how much they could get away with. In fact, the boy had unfailingly captured the rapt attention of every woman in the classroom—except for Lila.

On the other hand, Jack did know about men being one himself, and he knew exactly what was going on behind those young blue eyes as they roamed over the good doctor's body. Sex, and the cocky assurance that he could back up any promises he cared to make. This kid made Trey Farris look like a monk.

"Oh, hello, Ace," Lila said. "No, I'm afraid I'm not teaching this class."

Ace? Jack almost groaned.

"Too bad," Ace drawled, giving it everything he had. "We sure had a good time last semester."

Jack saw her quizzical look, the furrowing of her brow. "Didn't you flunk my class last semester?" she asked.

"Sure." A wide grin split the boy's classically handsome face. "But that doesn't mean I didn't have fun." With a wink and a swagger of lean hips in those tight jeans, Ace turned down one of the aisles of desks.

"I don't get it," she murmured, finally deigning to look at Jack. "He even came to my study group. I've never had anyone who came to study group fail my class."

Jack got it, and he started to tell her, his voice slightly strained due to the tightness of his jaw. "I think it was a concentration problem. With him concentrating too much on getting into your—"

"Dr. Singer! Hey! This is great!"

They both turned in the direction of the door and the well-groomed young man entering the room. Frat boy, Jack thought with a silent, re-signed sigh, taking in the expensive cut and cloth of the boy's suit and tie. Probably class president, or head of the Young Republicans Club. His blond hair was styled short and correct, and he had the look of somebody who was up and coming.

"Hello, Porter," she answered.

Porter? "Do you know all of your students by name?" Jack asked, not bothering to mask his irritation.

"Only the ones who drop by my office a lot, or those who are active in class discussion."

Why in the hell, Jack wondered, had he come to the university that day? To rub salt in his own wound? He'd had her in his bed for all of a morning and half of an afternoon and she'd taken a powder on him. What did he think he was going to prove in this den of overstimulated hormones?

"Are you teaching this class?" Porter asked.

"No," Lila repeated. "I just finished the last one."

"Are you going to be in your office later?" Porter directed the question to Lila, but his attention flickered over to Jack for a quick sizing-up moment.

"No," Jack said.

"Yes," Lila said at the same time.

They turned to look at each other, one face upturned and flushed, the other stoically determined.

Jack knew it was time to back off, but he had too much at stake, too much ego, too much future, too much of his heart.

"The lady in the office said you were finished teaching for the day," he said to Lila half under his breath, trying to keep the frat boy out of the conversation.

"I am," she said, her own voice soft, her eyes wide and unsure. "But I usually keep office hours on Wednesday afternoons."

"I'd like to come by and see you," Porter interjected.

Jack sighed again. What was the younger generation coming to? Didn't anybody respect their elders anymore? Or have enough sense to know when they were trespassing? Or was he the one out of line? Looking into Lila's eyes, he couldn't tell whose side she was on. But he knew he hadn't walked out of a job on a half-million-dollar house just to get shot down.

"I submitted that political science paper for publication, like you suggested," Porter said.

breaking the moment of silence. "I thought we could get together and talk about it some more."

"Sure," Lila tore her gaze away from Jack to address her student. Jack felt the effort it cost her, and though it didn't make sense, his confidence rebounded. Maybe her only problem was confusion. Lord knew, he was confused.

"I guess I can go back to work," he said, reaching out to cup her chin in his palm. He turned her until her eyes locked onto his and he had her undivided attention. "I get off at five and I'll be at your house by six." He gently tilted her face upward and whispered as his mouth descended to hers, "Be there, Lila."

She could have moved. She had time, and she knew what he was going to do long seconds before their lips met, long seconds before hers parted for the sweet invasion of his tongue. She didn't move, though, and in an instant she was swept back to Sunday morning, to the warmth and strength of his embrace, to the secret enticements of his mouth.

Had anyone ever kissed her with such passion, with such need? she wondered. With such cataclysmic results?

A shockwave of desire ripped through her, and her body automatically responded. Of its own accord, her fingers threaded through the hair at the nape of his neck, holding him to her. Her breasts yearned to be crushed against his chest. Her hips longed for the molding caress of his hands. Within the magical web of his kiss, she wanted more, always more, even though she knew they should stop.

"Neanderthal, man." She heard the unsolicited opinion from afar.

"*I* think it's romantic," a female voice responded.

Lila herself thought the heated kiss was crazy, and wild, and wonderful, and unorthodox, and was probably going to be a major source of embarrassment later. It could be dangerous to enjoy kissing Jack so much, especially if her department head found out.

Her mouth stilled. Her hand dropped away.

Jack understood her withdrawal and released her. But he did it slowly, kissing the corner of her mouth, then her cheek, before whispering in her ear, "Six o'clock."

Lila watched him leave, once again blissfully unaware of the students staring at her, until a quiet voice of indeterminate gender spoke from the back of the room.

"Sex education? Is this sex education? I didn't think they had sex education in college. And live models? I'm not sure I should be here."

Finally, she found the presence of mind to be embarrassed and hurried from the room.

Fifteen minutes to six. She'd changed her mind and her outfit eight times since she'd gotten home. She'd settled on staying put, and on a white blouse with a high collar, an ebony and gold brooch closing the neck, and a black split skirt with buff-leather-trimmed pockets and a buff-colored leather belt. Her boots matched the belt and trim. She felt her decisions on the outfit were pretty solid. Staying home to meet him, though, was still a long shot.

But they had to talk. That much was obvious even to her cowardly heart. She was a mature, grown woman, capable of reason. As a step in the right direction, she'd started a couple of lists of topics, good and bad. There had been little else to do during the past three nights of blanket twisting and pillow bashing. She hadn't intended to share her list of problems, excuses, and apologies— always an apology—but he was coming, and she doubted if he wanted to talk about two-by-fours and paint chips.

She looked at the kitchen clock again. Ten minutes to six. It was run now or hold her ground.

Five minutes to six. Jack pulled up in her driveway and was eternally grateful to see her car parked behind the house. In his experience, women didn't respond well to ultimatums. Not that he'd given many, or even cared to.

Lila was different, though. He had a list of dos and don'ts for her a mile long and no reason whatsoever to believe she'd follow any of them.

First of all, he thought she should be teaching kindergarten, not college. Actually, he thought she should be teaching kindergarten boys. She could teach all the girls of any age she wanted. College boys had too many ideas to suit him, from the insipid Trey Farris, to the cocky Ace, to the preppy Porter. The lady obviously had no idea of the broad base of her appeal. With so many men after her, it was a miracle she'd ended up with only one affair.

He did not count himself as an affair. He wasn't

giving up that easily or walking away with that little. He'd found something special in her. She had her feet on the ground, her life in order, and yet she retained a special innocence that was incredibly appealing. That first time he'd kissed her, he'd felt a pull on his soul, a need to touch her and share the magic surrounding her.

Danny had seen it. He'd capitalized his fame on the shimmering aura of Lila Singer. Jack wanted to capitalize on it, too, in the most personal ways imaginable. He wanted her inspiration for his own. He wanted to love and protect her and give her his heart in return.

He took a deep breath and looked out his windshield at the softly lit house. All he had to do was convince her to give him a chance. What the hell, he thought. At this point he'd settle for half a chance.

The ringing of the doorbell startled Lila into jumping off the barstool by the breakfast counter. The chair fell over and she scrambled for a minute to set it aright. She hadn't expected him to use the front door. She wondered what it meant.

Probably nothing, she admonished herself. He was just being polite.

She smoothed her culottes and straightened the placket on her blouse. He was just being polite, she repeated silently. Or was he being formal? And how did she fit formality into an evening with the man she'd spent a morning making love with just before she'd ran off?

Life had been so simple before Christmas Eve. Why had she gone and made it all messy and complicated and full of possibilities and promise?

She stopped in front of a gilt-framed rococo mirror in the hall and ran her fingers through her hair, fluffing the curls into place. Large eyes stared back at her.

"Why couldn't you stay out of trouble for one more day?" she whispered to her image. "Was that too much to ask?"

Yes, her heart answered, and it might have told her more, but the doorbell rang again.

After a calming breath, she took the necessary four steps to the door and opened it.

He looked great, better than great. He looked like everything she'd ever dreamed of in a man, and a lover, and a mate. She was hopeless.

"Hi."

"Hi," he echoed with the slightest smile curving his mouth.

It took her a moment to absorb the smile and the warmth of his gaze, but as soon as she did, she remembered to invite him inside.

"Come in . . . please," she said, making a welcoming gesture and moving out of the way.

As he stepped by her, she did a completely unpremeditated and purely subjective appraisal of him, her gaze skimming him from top to bottom. Dove-gray jeans encased his long legs, ending at cream-colored cowboy boots tipped in dark brown that had seen their share of wear. The jeans were worn, too, giving them a soft sheen, and she fleetingly thought about brushing her fingers across them.

She quickly clutched her hands together and waited while he shrugged out of his leather jacket.

The action revealed a black chamois shirt and brought to mind a similar movement he'd made on Sunday when he'd bared his chest.

When, she wondered in silent irritation, had she slipped into such a sophomoric, one-track frame of mind? There had never been another time in her life when so many of her thoughts had revolved around sex and the male body. She certainly hadn't had such thoughts about Robert, which might explain why the one time she had gone to bed with him she'd cried through most of it and enjoyed none of it.

"Something smells great," he said, laying his jacket across a chair arm.

"Oh, yes, well, I whipped up a little dinner." She stuck a smile on her face to cover her lie. She hadn't whipped anything up. What she'd done was re-whip what her mother had served her the previous night. She didn't know if she was trying to impress him, save him the cost of another night out, or ensure a modicum of privacy for their talk. Whatever their talk turned out to be about, she was sure they'd need at least a modicum of privacy, maybe more.

"If I'd known," he said, "I would have brought some wine."

"I have wine," she assured him. In truth, she was already on her second glass. It was supposed to calm her nerves, but it hadn't.

The awkwardness of the moment increased exponentially for every tenth of a second she spent looking up at him, until it reached the unbearable point.

"Well, yes," she managed to choke out, her gaze

dropping to her eye level and his chest. "Why don't we go ahead and eat."

That wasn't right, she thought. She knew that wasn't right. People were supposed to chat before dinner, not drop their coats and chow down.

Things had definitely gotten worse. If he'd never kissed her, she might have maintained her control. But he'd kissed her right off the bat, less than half an hour after a very polite business introduction, and things had been going downhill ever since. Leaping into bed with him had only quadrupled the speed of her slide into chaos.

Hc followed her into the dining room, while she tried to fit in some cocktail conversation.

"How long have you been doing sculpture?" A great question, she praised herself, but she should have asked it days before. At the time they'd both had something else on their minds, though.

"I had an art teacher in high school," he said. "He also doubled as the remedial reading teacher. We spent a lot of time together, mostly in a stand-off, or with him sending me to study hall or giving me detentions, until I finally broke him. Do you need some help?" he asked.

"Please," she replied, leading the way into the kitchen. "Broke him?"

"One day he just got fed up. He snapped, threw a book at me, bounced it off my head. Sure got my attention."

She gave him a concerned look as she handed him a pair of potholders. "Did he lose his job?"

"Nobody ever knew."

"You didn't report him?" She opened the oven and pointed to the two casserole dishes. "They both need to be set on the table."

"Nah. I was a cocky little jerk. He should have kicked my butt a lot sooner. His name was Art. Get it?"

"Art the art teacher?"

"We called him Art-Art."

She lifted the salad bowl out of the refrigerator, shaking her head. "You must have been a terror, a teacher's nightmare."

He shrugged. "There wasn't a lot in school to hold my interest, not until Art taught me how to weld coat hangers together."

"You two became friends?"

"I wouldn't go that far. Let's say we decided not to waste each other's time in the reading lab. When it was just the two of us, we hid out in the shop."

As he carried the second casserole dish into the dining room, Lila took the bread out of the oven and arranged it in a linen-lined basket.

"This stuff really does smell great," he said, lifting the lid off one of the hot dishes. "And it looks great. I love spaghetti. What's this other one called?"

Lila hesitated for a moment in the kitchen, her hand resting on the bread basket. She didn't make the stuff, or call it by name. She just heated it up. "Uh . . . it's an old family recipe, made with eggplant."

"Looks great," he repeated.

She let out a sigh of relief. He didn't want details.

"Maybe you could give me the recipe."

He wanted details, probably more than she had. Her total set of instructions consisted of "one half hour at three fifty."

"Sure," she said, grabbing the bread basket and walking into the dining room, determined to change the subject before they got to the point where she was sneaking off to her bedroom to call her mother.

"So," she began after they were seated. "You started out welding coat hangers. When did you graduate to half a ton of steel?"

Eleven

". . . And after I'd welded up all the rusty junk
lying around my dad's farm, I started looking for
something new and shiny, like steel." He glanced
up from his plate, grinning. "Over the last couple
of years the pieces have gotten bigger and bigger, a
lot bigger than I ever thought they'd get. I finally
had to build the garage."

"Have you ever shown your work?" Lila asked
learning forward with her hand cupped in her
chin. She'd become so fascinated by his story
she'd forgotten to be nervous.

"A couple of people here and there have seen a
few of my sculptures," he said, shrugging nonchal
lantly. "It's not something I do for other people."

"And it's not a hobby," she added, remembering
his reply to her question on the subject a couple of
weeks earlier.

"No." He grinned again, pouring himself more
wine. "It's not a hobby."

"Still, I bet you could sell some of the pieces, especially your bronze work."

"My bronze work?" He quirked an eyebrow.

"Sure," she said, getting excited. "Even people without an eye for art, real art, like your phoenix in the garage, go for bronze castings." Danny had never considered a photograph complete until someone paid him. It was a measure of success, he'd said. Not necessarily the most important one, but a vital one.

"Bronze castings," Jack murmured, pouring the last of the wine into his glass and setting the bottle aside. Suddenly he laughed. "You mean the mermaid?"

No, she hadn't meant the mermaid. She wouldn't have deliberately mentioned that particular piece. She had assumed he must have more bronzes of different subjects. "Well, yes . . . or something else like it."

He shook his head, still laughing. "Oh, there's nothing else quite like the mermaid."

She silently agreed as she drank the rest of her wine. Few women were built like his ex-wife. It bothered the hell out of her, even though she knew comparisons were ridiculous, unnecessary, unhealthy, and oh so human.

"Even if I did bronzes," he continued, "I doubt if I could come up with something quite as . . ." He paused, searching for a word. "Quite as *blatant* as a half-naked woman decked out as a mermaid. From the day it arrived, I always felt it lacked a certain subtlety of style, a certain refinement of spirit. But you're right. The stuff sells like hotcakes. I've heard the artist does quite well for himself in California."

"California?"

"Yeah, his name is Rico. It took me a long time to figure out why he sent it to me. Christina and I had been divorced for over a year when it came, so it was a little late to make me jealous. But then, it was always a little late to make me jealous where Christina was concerned."

"Oh?" Lila said, dying of curiosity, but not wanting it to show. It struck her that in all their time together, the heart-to-heart confessions had always come from her. She knew virtually nothing about the ups and downs of his emotional life.

Their eyes met across the table and the two candles she'd lit for no special reason, certainly not to create a romantic atmosphere. He held her gaze for a long, quiet moment.

"I guess this is part of what we need to talk about," he said softly.

She nodded, not trusting herself to speak.

"It must have been pretty awful for you to find her in the house Sunday afternoon."

She nodded again and wondered if maybe it wasn't absolutely necessary for them to talk about this after all.

"I mean," he went on, "there were still four cookies left, and you left all of them for me without a word." He grinned a little grin, deepening the crease in one cheek. "I figured something pretty terrible must have scared you off."

She lowered her gaze to her plate.

"Christina's timing has always been bad," he continued. "She started sleeping with old Rico weeks before she remembered to tell me she wanted a divorce."

Lila's head snapped up. Jack wasn't smiling anymore.

"It happens." He shrugged and took another swallow of wine. After setting the glass back down, he twirled it between his fingers. "The trick is making sure it doesn't happen to you."

"I'm sorry," she whispered.

"Don't be," he replied evenly, glancing up at her. "I'm not."

"But you must have loved her."

"I wanted her. There's a difference."

The words were spoken slowly, but they made her heart race with something akin to panic. She knew there was a difference, and she was afraid that wanting had more to do with what was between them than loving, more afraid than she'd realized until he'd said the words aloud.

She rose abruptly. "I'll get dessert. We're having a cake, chocolate. Cheesecake actually. A chocolate cheesecake."

In the kitchen, she set her plate in the sink and grasped the edge of the counter with both hands. Her chin lowered to her chest, and she squeezed her eyes shut.

Jack had followed her, and he now stood in the archway between the kitchen and the dining room, studying her bowed head and the dark curls falling around her neck and shoulders. She was very still, with her knee bent and the toe of one boot resting behind the heel of the other. But the tension emanating from her slender form was undeniable. He felt it across the width of the kitchen.

"If you'd give me some guidelines," he said, "maybe I could stop saying the wrong thing." He spoke lightly, but he was damn serious. She was like water running through his hands, an ethereal mist he couldn't catch in his fingers. Every time he thought he had her, she slipped away. Her husband probably hadn't had to do anything special to her to make his photograph. She *was* the queen of the woodland fairies—a dream impossible to hold on to.

"It's not you," she said, lifting her head and pretending to be doing something in the sink. She didn't fool Jack.

"If it's Christina, or the mermaid, they're both gone. That's why she came back, to get the mermaid. Apparently, she's running a little low on cash, and Rico had told her he'd sent a copy of the sculpture to me in a fit of remorse. Sort of a let-bygones-be-bygones gesture after she left him. She figured I didn't really want it, and she was right."

"Must have left a big empty spot in your bathroom," she said.

"Actually, it kind of helped the place. I gave her the copper seaweed too." At her lack of response, he continued talking, pausing occasionally in case she had something to add to the conversation. "One of these days, I'll get around to chipping out all those seashells . . . should have done it a long time ago. Christina and I never did have the same taste in interior—"

"It's not Christina or the mermaid," she interrupted, turning to face him. "It's you and me together."

He mulled her statement over for a couple of seconds, then said, "I like you and me together."

"So do I," she admitted. "Maybe too much."

He was starting to get confused again, and he didn't know if he should keep that news flash to himself or tell her. He chose a roundabout route. "How about Sunday? Did you like us too much on Sunday?"

Predictably, the color rose in her cheeks, and she nodded. "Far too much."

"Good," he said quickly. At least he hadn't been wrong about that. He began to feel better—until she spoke.

"We've been far too physically attracted to each other from the beginning."

"I like physical attraction," he countered, feeling himself losing ground. He hastily tried to shore up his case. "I like it a lot, especially with you. As a matter of fact, I don't remember ever liking physical attraction as much as I liked it on Sunday."

"Me either," she confessed.

He took a step forward, but her next words stopped him.

"And I think it's a very shaky basis for a relationship."

"Well," he improvised slowly, taking another step, "so do I, but I think . . . I *know* we have more in common than physical attraction."

"Not much," she said, her voice taking on a resigned tone as she dug into her skirt pocket. "I made a list, and it's darned short."

"A list?"

She sorted through the scraps of paper in her pocket and shot him a quick glance. "Sex and chocolate."

Sounded good to him.

"And art," she added. "Or, rather, you have an interest in art, and I seem to have a subconscious interest in artists, since I was obviously attracted to you before I knew you were a metal sculptor."

He didn't know what to say. Unfortunately, she did.

"It's not enough, Jack."

Why not? he wanted to know, but he phrased his question differently. "How many things in common would be enough?"

"Enough for what?"

She was getting quick, he thought, momentarily caught off guard. He wanted enough things to get her back in bed, that was for sure. But he also wanted enough things to get himself an open invitation to dinner, and breakfast, and lunch. He was tired of eating alone, and if tonight was any indication, she could cook circles around him.

He wanted enough things so that his heart didn't go into cardiac arrest every time he got close to her, for fear she'd skip out on him. He wanted enough things to make her happy, to light her face with a sweet glow of contentment . . . forever.

"Enough for marriage," he said, not surprising himself, but shocking the daylights out of her.

"Marriage?" she gasped, one hand landing on her chest.

"Yes. Despite one not-so-good try at it, I still like marriage. I believe in it, and I think you do too. Please add that to your list."

Lila stared at him in amazement. With three short words he'd catapulted their relationship into the stratosphere. The man didn't know when to quit. First, he'd kissed her when he had no business doing any such thing. Then he'd slipped inside her life until they'd actually had a dinner date. Worse yet, he'd made himself utterly irresist ible. She'd practically chased him into bed. Now he was talking about the ultimate commitment, the lifetime, through sickness and health, till-death-do-us-part type of relationship that she'd thrived on with Danny.

It still shocked her.

"I . . ." she began, but got no further. She tried again. "I . . ."

"How many things would that take, Lila?" he asked, moving one step closer, then another. "How many?"

"Umm . . ." She closed her eyes for a quick second, trying to think. But it was impossible to think when he was moving in on her. "Ten . . . or—or twelve," she said breathlessly. Her eyes popped open in the nick of time to keep him from kissing her and completely undermining her good intentions. "Maybe twenty, or twenty-five, or fifty. I don't know. I never thought of it in those terms."

Her head was tilted up to keep him in sight, and he wondered if she knew her neck was one of his favorite erogenous zones.

"Well, let's think about it for a minute," he said, letting his natural drawl smooth out the thought and slow down the words. "We've already got sex, chocolate, art, and marriage. Seems like a pretty good start. And let's go with your first estimation, ten things. Now I'm going to add quality construction to make five, since we both have shown uncommon interest in quality construction. That leaves five things to go. I think we can come up with five things." In five minutes or less, he figured. Then they could get on to the first two things, something chocolate for dessert after din-

ner, and some kind of sex for dessert after chocolate. He had a lot of ideas.

"It's not that simple, Jack. It can't be. Relation-
ships take time, nurturing, structure, a support
network of values and interests, a—"

"How long did you know your husband before
you married him?" he interrupted, then winced.
Lord, he hated bringing the guy up.

"Two months."

"Case closed." And that would be the last time he
reminded her that she'd loved someone before she
loved him, he silently added, because he knew she
loved him. She'd erased his doubts on Sunday. All
he had to do was erase hers.

"But—"

"Five things," he said, holding up his hand with
fingers spread. "Give me a chance. I know I can do
this."

And he would have, that very night, if she hadn't
come up with her own set of restrictions. All
things of common interest had to be matters of
consequence. She would let him get away with
quality construction, but nothing else in a similar
vein would count. They'd both agreed, after a
couple of bites of her mother's chocolate cheesecake, that chocolate didn't suffer from the same
lack of importance. Lila accepted all compliments
on dinner and dessert with hardly a trace of guilt
but balked at adding Italian food to the list. It was
obvious, she'd said, that between the two of them
they'd eat anything that didn't eat them first.

Then she'd gotten serious, painfully serious.

"Given the combustibility of our reaction to each

other, I think it best if we refrain from . . . refrain from . . ." Words had failed her, but Jack got the point.

"Sex," he said, filling in the blank. Then he wished he'd tried something else first, just in case.

"Yes," she said, blowing out his last hope. "If you want to give this relationship a chance, I think we should try keeping company for a while."

"Keeping company?" He thought he knew what the term meant, but a little clarification couldn't hurt.

"Yes. See each other occasionally. Date, if you will."

"I will."

"Talk about things, get to know each other."

He nodded at every suggestion she made, trying to be agreeable, but he already knew things about her that made it impossible to sleep at night: how she felt in his arms, warm, soft, supple, sleek; the taste of her on his lips; the scent of her.

He was back at her door the next night. If they were going to keep company, he'd decided not to waste time by waiting for the weekend. She'd ended the previous evening without so much as a kiss. He was determined to do better that night. Besides, he'd come up with another item for her list.

She opened the door, and his jaw went slack. He didn't believe she had a cruel streak, but neither could he believe what she was wearing. Or rather, what she wasn't wearing.

"You're early," she said, her voice slightly breathless. Big clips pinned her hair in a lush disarray on top of her head. Moisture dampened her throat and the bared slope of one shoulder. A short robe of black silk splashed with white camelias clung to her breasts and her hips, barely holding on, barely covering.

"Or late," he muttered, letting his gaze roam at will, letting his memory conjure up the indelible image hidden by the scrap of silk.

"Come in, please, before we both freeze to death."

He didn't want to disappoint her, but truthfully, he was in no danger of freezing to death.

"Oh, Jack. They're beautiful." Her eyes lit up when she saw the flowers he'd brought. He thought they ran a poor second to the camelias caressing the creamy softness of her skin.

"Tiger lilies," he said, closing the door behind him.

"Thank you." She gathered the huge bouquet into her arms and padded into the kitchen, with Jack just far enough behind to catch every sweet sway of her hips.

When she reached up into a cupboard to get a large glass vase, he vowed to bring her flowers every night. Then he grinned and ran a hand through his hair, shaking his head in disbelief. He used to think he was a classy guy, a man of integrity, but she brought out his primitive side, his primal masculine instincts. Instincts of capture and conquering, of baring her body to his gaze and taking her. He ought to be shot as a reprobate.

But no one was going to shoot anybody, and he wasn't about to strip her clothes off at this point, so he looked his fill and enjoyed the heightened awareness of his senses, the waywardness of his imagination, and the initial stirrings of arousal. He was a man in love.

"It'll take me only a minute to finish getting ready," she said, running water in the vase and casting him a glance over her shoulder. She quickly pulled the silk collar up, and it just as quickly slipped back down.

"No hurry," he assured her, not even trying to resist the urge to touch her. With a sure hand he arranged the robe over her shoulder and felt the unmistakable warmth of her response. "I thought we'd try the Mexican place in the alley over behind the bank."

"I've been there. It's great." She bent her head over the tiger lilies in mock concentration as she cut the end off the stem of each flower.

"Yeah, he said softly, letting his hand drift down her arm. "Really great."

What did he think she was made of? Lila wondered. Steel? Well, she wasn't, and she couldn't take much more.

Whirling around, she confronted him. "You're cheating again."

A smile eased across his face, and his gaze fixed deliberately on the opening of her robe. "So are you. Not that I mind."

She wasn't mad. She was too breathless to be mad. "I'll be ready in a minute."

Clutching her robe together, she practically ran out of the kitchen, his words echoing behind her.

"I think we better count cheating, Lila. That's a pretty important thing to know about each other."

Jack grinned to himself. He was batting a thousand. He'd gotten the list up to six things, and he hadn't even sprung the item he'd spent half the night lying awake to dream up.

"Another margarita, please," Lila said to the hovering waitress, and wondered for the millionth time if she'd overdressed for Mexican food. Her dress was a slinky rayon with tiny green and black checks, padded shoulders, a sarong-style skirt, and a self belt. Everybody else in the place was wearing jeans.

Jack sat quietly until the waitress left, helping himself to salsa and chips while she finished delivering their dinner. He'd felt only the tiniest twinge of guilt as Lila had read the menu to him. She'd done it so professionally, her Spanish accent equal to her French. He'd already decided to take her out for Chinese to see what happened.

"And more sour cream, please," she continued, adding to her order.

"I'll have another beer."

"And a side of guacamole."

"Maybe we should go into the restaurant business together," he said. "That would make seven."

Lila shifted her attention to him, and the waitress slipped away while there was a lull in the barrage of requests.

"I'm disqualifying number six," she whispered leaning across the table. "I *was not* deliberately trying to seduce you. You were early."

"You knew it was me," he countered. "You could have put a blanket over your head."

"I was *fixing* my hair," she insisted. "And if hadn't known for sure it was you, I wouldn't have answered the door at all."

"You're shy. I'm shy too. That makes eight."

"Six."

"We'll compromise. Seven."

"Fine." She sat back with a small huff, knowing she'd never win the battle.

"We're capable of negotiating to a satisfactory conclusion. That makes nine."

"Eight."

"Okay." He grinned. "See how easy it is."

She shook her head, then leveled him with her steady gaze. "You are not shy. Seven."

"I'm not shy with you," he corrected her. "But you should have seen me on my last blind date. It was a disaster, bona fide, guaranteed."

"Blind date?" she questioned, one silky brow arching.

"Yeah. Smitty set me up with a friend of his cousin's. She was a real nice lady, but . . ." He left the word hanging in air, his gaze suddenly turning thoughtful.

"But?" Lila prompted, curious as all get out and not even attempting to hide it.

He remained silent for another moment, then said softly, "But she wasn't you, Lila. I'd met you only an hour before I picked her up, and it was already too late. I was already in over my head. I was already in love. I know that sounds crazy, but I think sometimes it happens that way. One minute your life is rolling along like it always does, and the next, someone looks at you with moonlight in her hair and magic happens. Your heartbeat quickens, your energy focuses, the rest of the world drops out of sight, until there's only the most beautiful woman you've ever seen standing before you and a compulsion older than man to take her and make her yours. I don't claim to understand it, but I have to believe it, because it happened to me once, last September, under the cottonwood trees in your driveway."

Lila listened, enraptured, her jealousy melting away.

"Oh, Jack," she whispered, reaching across the table for his hand.

"I like my job," he said, holding her fingers in the warmth of his palm, his thumb caressing her skin. Do you like yours?"

"Yes."

"Nine."

"Nine," she said simultaneously.

The flourish of a cocktail napkin drew their attention to the waitress.

"Fresh drinks," she said with a bright smile. "Is everything okay?"

Lila's gaze dropped to her plate of untouched food, and Jack said, "Can you wrap all of this to go?"

"Uh . . . sure," the waitress replied.

"Great," Lila said, scooting away from the table.

"Could you add something chocolate for dessert to the order?" Jack asked while he shrugged into his jacket. "We'll meet you at the cashier's desk."

"Uh . . . sure," the waitress repeated, though she looked less than one hundred percent positive.

"Great," he said with a megawatt smile.

They held hands all the way home, except when he needed to shift gears, but his hand always came back to hers.

He wanted to say something like *Don't let me rush you into anything. Or I'll stay up all night long and come up with stuff to put on your list, if you like, but it won't make any difference. No difference at all in how I feel.*

But all he did was hold her hand and try not to smile himself right off the map.

Twelve

They carried their dinner into her kitchen, their hands full. Jack was cruising on "full speed ahead," but Lila had turned into all thumbs and nerves. She barely made it to the counter before her packages slipped away from her.

"Oops." She lunged for the paper cup full of guacamole, inadvertently spilling it into her hand and across the top of another package. "Darn," she cussed under her breath, and licked one finger off while reaching for a paper towel.

She didn't get close to the roll. Warm masculine hands wrapped around both of her wrists, and while he helped himself to a long lick of guacamole, he took her other hand and pressed it to his abdomen.

His eyes burned down into hers, and his tongue did crazy things to the sensitive skin of her palm, making it impossible to catch her breath.

"Spicy," he murmured between licks, and she

could only nod. He released her other hand and pulled his shirt out of his pants until her fingers nested in soft hair and on hot skin.

He wasn't shy, she thought. No shy person could ever do what he was doing to her, a fact confirmed in her mind when he sucked her finger into his mouth and sent a flood of heat pouring down her body. She wanted to kiss him so badly she ached.

"Jack." His name whispered from her lips and her eyes closed on a sigh.

He didn't disappoint her. His mouth came down on hers, gentle but insistent, and all-consuming. This was no mere kiss, but a prelude to loving like they'd shared on Sunday. With each stroke of his tongue he reminded her of every sweet thrill to come, of every nuance to be anticipated and enjoyed.

Her hands explored his chest, reveling in the feel of him, in the memories his body brought back. She moaned into his mouth and started a chain reaction of sensual magic. His hands dropped to her hips, and her dress slowly bunched up under his fingers.

"I missed you," he murmured between sultry, drugging kisses.

"You saw me last night," she eventually responded, unbuttoning his shirt with unsteady hands. She stretched up on tiptoe to savor more fully the taste and heat of his mouth, the skill of his methods. She hadn't known anyone could put so much into a kiss.

"I've missed you since Sunday," he broke off long enough to say, then seared a path down to the pulse point of her throat while his hand slipped down one thigh and then up the other.

"Gracious," she gasped as she felt her garter snaps give way in sequence.

He swung her up into his arms, then carried her out of the kitchen and down the hall.

"The food—" she started.

"Will keep," he finished, stepping sideways through her bedroom door.

He'd seen the room a few times on his way back and forth from the bathroom, but he'd never lingered overlong in the hall. It was better to be invited.

Draperies of heavy lace covered the tall windows. Flowered wallpaper in shades of rose, mauve, and lavender gave the room a special feminine intimacy and warmth. Jack liked being there, in the inner sanctum where she dreamed her private dreams. He liked the scent of her perfume in the air. He looked at the bed and grinned. He liked knowing she'd tried on half a dozen outfits before she'd decided on the slinky green dress.

"You're sweet," he whispered in her ear, and stole a kiss, teasing her skin right where he knew he'd get the maximum effect.

"You're shameless," she whispered back, arching her neck to give him greater access.

"No. I'm in love."

"Me too."

His mouth stilled on her skin, and he slowly lifted his head, a questioning look in his eyes. Lila met his gaze steadily, knowing she'd already stepped over the line. What had she found in this man? she wondered. He held her with care, not only in his arms, but in his heart. He'd been gentle and kind, and seductive . . . so wonderfully seductive, slipping into her life and her heart with barely a ripple, as if they'd been made for each other and had only been waiting for the right time, for a harvest moon on a crisp autumn night, to fill the air with magic. He was the good man she needed.

"That makes ten, Lila," he told her.

"That makes ten," she said with a warm smile, then pulled his mouth down to hers.

"He's *gorgeous*!" Didi exclaimed, grabbing Lila's arm. "Aren't you just full of surprises? Jack Hudson. Who would have guessed your dyslexic Jack Hudson was the same Jack Hudson my husband has been talking about all these months? His diamond in the rough. His 'some guy out on a farm east of here doing incredible stuff with steel.'" Didi paused for a rare breath, and her gaze zeroed back in on the two men talking by the huge sculpture on display in the towering lobby. "Who would have thought he looked like that?"

"It's not a farm," Lila corrected her friend, a little unnerved by all the attention Jack was receiving from the female part of the party. With Kevin acting as his broker, Jack had sold his phoenix sculpture to an international manufacturing firm based in Denver. He'd had the most amazing reaction to it, too, one Lila was still trying to figure out. "And what do you mean, looks like that?" she asked. "He looks like everybody else, perfectly ordinary."

"Sure, honey." Didi laughed. "He's just got ordinary down in a very sexy, extraordinary way. You should have told me."

"Why?" she asked absently, her gaze still fixed on Jack.

"Because I've been worrying about you for too long not to be informed of every turnabout in your love life. You keep too much to yourself."

Lila frowned as she watched a ravishing redhead sidle up to Jack and actually touch his arm. "What is she doing?"

"Jealousy. I like that."

"I'm serious, Didi. What does she think she's doing?"

"Only what every woman in the room wants to do, honey. She's making her play."

"And what am I supposed to do about it?" A tightness crept into her voice, eliciting a pair of raised eyebrows from her friend.

"Well, the Lila I used to know probably wouldn't have done anything except suffer in silence, but I've got a feeling the new Lila is a woman of action." Didi finished that sentence without an audience.

Lila made a beeline for Jack, Kevin, the sculpture, and the redhead. The white dinner jacket with black slacks was too much. She'd known it the minute he'd slipped the suit on. No sane woman could resist him in a white dinner jacket.

Jack caught sight of her heading his way, and he quickly excused himself from Kevin and the public relations lady who'd been stalking him all night long. From the look on Lila's face, he figured she must have noticed the redhead too. If she knew how little reason she had to be jealous of anyone, he'd be putty in her hands. Which, on second thought, didn't sound like such a bad idea.

Lord, she looked beautiful tonight. She'd gotten her hair, which wasn't actually long, to pile up on top of her head. He couldn't wait to run his hands through it and pull it all back down. Her dress should have been outlawed. Royal blue sequins shimmered down the front, down her arms, and across the discreet, high-necked collar. They hugged the slender curves of her hips in unadorned simplicity. But the dress was very much like the woman who wore it, prim and proper on the face of it, and wonderfully uninhibited on the other side. There was no back, not until past the curve of her waist. She wouldn't have lasted two minutes in that den of oversexed males called a university. Fortunately, the older corporate crowd was more subtle, though hardly less dangerous. He hadn't taken his eyes off her the whole night.

"Had enough?" he asked, reaching for her hand.

His question brought Lila up short even as his arm drew her near. There it was again, she thought, his amazing reaction. Danny hadn't exactly been a media hound, but he'd played every bit of promotion for all it was worth. Jack, on the other hand, was more inclined in the other direction. He gave "laid back" a whole new meaning.

"Well, yes," she said. "But have you?"

He gave the room a thoughtful glance before looking back at her. "Yeah," he said with a grin. "I think the excitement has worn down enough for me to tear myself away."

She had to ask. It was driving her crazy not to know. "Isn't all this important to you?"

"Sure. It's great, a thrill, but the hoopla is almost over and you made a promise to me last week, one I'm holding you to."

She couldn't stop her impish smile, but she did try for a reproachful tone. "That promise is for tomorrow morning, and you know I'm not going to back out on you."

"You're not going to get a chance," he informed her, a sultry light in his eye. "I've got plans for you, woman. Private plans."

"You're bad, Jack Hudson," she whispered, trying not to giggle. "All these people are here to pay homage to you, and you're thinking about—"

"The really important stuff. Are you packed?"

"I have been for a week, as you very well know." They'd been living out of two houses for a month, which was four weeks longer than Jack had liked.

"Did you remember to put in the black outfit I bought you?"

"Outfit?" She shot him a scandalized look. "By no stretch of the imagination is that scrap of black lace an *outfit*. It barely qualifies as a nightie."

"Right." He grinned. "We're going to have fun."

"I'll probably freeze to death," she said with a petulance he found particularly endearing on her sweet mouth. She'd changed into an unmerciful tease over the past weeks, revealing a playful side he doubted many people had ever seen, and he loved it.

"Oh, no, honey," he said softly, pulling her into his arms and bending his head down to whisper in her ear. "I'm not going to let you get cold, not even close. We're probably going to melt snow down half the Vail valley."

"We could get arrested," she murmured, snuggling up closer.

"Nobody gets arrested on their honeymoon. I think it's against the law."

"So is making love in corporate lobbies," she teased.

"We're not making love."

"Not yet."

He stole a quick kiss off her cheek and almost lingered longer. She smelled so good and felt so soft.

"Lila, honey," he said, straightening away from her, but still holding her close. "There is one thing I think you ought to know before the wedding tomorrow morning."

"Oh?" She looked up at him, waiting.

"Yeah, well, I *can* read."

"Oh." Another mischievous smile curved her mouth. "Well, maybe there's something I ought to tell you."

"Like what?" he asked, his curiosity immediately on alert.

"I *can't* cook."

He gazed at her for a long moment, then calmly said, "I knew that."

"Impossible."

"No." He shook his head. "I knew. I swear."

"How?"

"Pots and pans. You don't seem to need them no matter what you serve for dinner. Nobody's freezer is that well stocked. I knew you had to have an outside source."

"Outside source?"

"Your mother."

She started to blush, but ended up laughing instead. "You're bad, Jack Hudson, leading me on with all those compliments. And you're the best." Her voice softened, and her hand found his. "You're the absolute best thing to ever happen to me. I never thought I'd love anybody the way I love you. I look at you and my heart flips right over. You kiss me and I come alive inside. I want to build dreams with you, yours and mine, and ours. I want us to last forever."

"I'm not going anywhere, Lila," he assured her with all the truth in his heart. "I'll still be with you when the moon catches silver in your hair."

"When I'm old and wrinkly?"

"And forgetful."

"And slow to get around?"

"And crabby."

"I'm not going to be crabby," she said, still intensely serious.

"Good." He kissed the frown off her brow. "You promise not to get crabby, and I'll promise not to get stubborn. Deal?"

"Deal," she said, slipping her hand around in his for a shake.

"Good." He grinned and headed for the outside door. "Now let's go home and make love before we both get too old and forgetful, and crabby and stubborn, to remember how to do it right."

"I'm sure we've got a few good years still in us," she said, her heels clicking rapidly with her effort to keep up with him.

"Yeah, but at this stage of the game, who wants to take any chances?"

He had a point, she thought. A darn good point. So she let him slip her mink over her shoulders, and she let him hold her hand on the drive home, and she loved him the whole night long . . . and as she slept within the circle of his arms, with his warm breath sighing across her skin, she dreamed of hazel eyes and gentle strength, of a man and a woman under a harvest moon, and of forever.

THE EDITOR'S CORNER

LOVESWEPT sails into autumn with six marvelous romances featuring passionate, independent, and truly remarkable heroines. And you can be sure they each find the wonderful heroes they deserve. With temperatures starting to drop and daylight hours becoming shorter, there's no better time to cuddle up with a LOVESWEPT!

Leading our lineup for October is **IN ANNIE'S EYES** by Billie Green, LOVESWEPT #504. This emotionally powerful story is an example of the author's great skill in touching our hearts. Max Decatur was her first lover and her only love, and marrying him was Anne Seaton's dream come true. But in a moment of confusion and sorrow she left him, believing she stood in the way of his promising career. Now after eleven lonely years he's back in her life, and she's ready to face his anger and furious revenge. Max waited forever to hurt her, but seeing her again ignites long-buried desire. And suddenly nothing matters but rekindling the old flame of passion. . . . An absolute winner!

Linda Cajio comes up with the most unlikely couple—and plenty of laughter—in the utterly enchanting **NIGHT MUSIC**, LOVESWEPT #505. Hilary Rayburn can't turn down Devlin Kitteridge's scheme to bring her grandfather and his matchmaking grandmother together more than sixty years after a broken engagement—even if it means carrying on a charade as lovers. Dev and Hilary have nothing in common but their plan, yet she can't catch her breath when he draws her close and kisses her into sweet oblivion. Dev wants no part of this elegant social butterfly—until he succumbs to her sizzling warmth and vulnerable softness. You'll be thoroughly entertained as these two couples find their way to happy-ever-after.

Many of you might think of that wonderful song "Some Enchanted Evening" when you read the opening scenes of **TO GIVE A HEART WINGS** by Mary Kay McComas, LOVESWEPT #506. For it is across a crowded room that Colt McKinnon first spots Hannah Alexander, and right away he knows he must claim her. When he takes her hand to dance and feels her body cleave to his with electric satisfaction, this daredevil racer finally believes in love at first sight. But when the music stops Hannah escapes before he can discover her secret pain. How is she to know that he would track her down, determined to possess her and slay her dragons? There's no resisting Colt's strong arms and tender smile, and finally Hannah discovers how wonderful it is to fly on the wings of love.

A vacation in the Caribbean turns into an exciting and passionate adventure in **DATE WITH THE DEVIL** by Olivia Rupprecht, LOVESWEPT #507. When prim and proper Diedre Forsythe is marooned on an island in the Bermuda Triangle with only martial arts master Sterling Jakes for a companion, she thinks she's in trouble. She doesn't expect the thrill of Sterling's survival training or his spellbinding seduction. Finally she throws caution to the wind and surrenders to the risky promise of his intimate caress. He's a man of secrets and shadows, but he's also her destiny, her soulmate. If they're ever rescued from their paradise, would her newfound courage be strong enough to hold him? This is a riveting story written with great sensuality.

The latest from Lori Copeland, **MELANCHOLY BABY**, LOVE-SWEPT #508, will have you sighing for its handsome hell-raiser of a hero. Bud Huntington was the best-looking boy in high school, and the wildest—but now the reckless rebel is the local doctor, and the most gorgeous man Teal Anderson has seen. She wants him as much as ever—and Bud knows it! He understands just how to tease the cool redhead, to stoke the flames of her long-suppressed desire with kisses that demand a lifetime commitment. Teal shook off the dust of her small Missouri hometown for the excitement of a big city years ago, but circumstances forced her to return, and now in Bud's arms she knows she'll never be a melancholy baby again. You'll be enthralled with the way these two confront and solve their problems.

There can't be a more appropriate title than **DANGEROUS PROPOSITION** for Judy Gill's next LOVESWEPT, #509. It's bad enough that widow Liss Tremayne has to drive through a blizzard to get to the cattle ranch she's recently inherited, but she knows when she gets there she'll be sharing the place with a man who doesn't want her around. Still, Liss will dare anything to provide a good life for her two young sons. Kirk Allbright has his own reasons for wishing Liss hasn't invaded his sanctuary: the feminine scent of her hair, the silky feel of her skin, the sensual glow in her dark eyes—all are perilous to a cowboy who finds it hard to trust anyone. But the cold ache in their hearts melts as warm winter nights begin to work their magic. . . . You'll relish every moment in this touching love story.

FANFARE presents four truly spectacular books next month! Don't miss out on **RENDEZVOUS**, the new and fabulous historical novel by bestselling author Amanda Quick: **MIRACLE,** an unforgettable contemporary story of love and the collision of two worlds, from critically acclaimed Deborah Smith: **CIRCLE OF PEARLS,** a thrilling historical by immensely talented Rosalind Laker; and **FOREVER,** by Theresa Weir, a heart-grabbing contemporary romance.

Happy reading!

With warmest wishes,

Nita Taublib

Nita Taublib
Associate Publisher/LOVESWEPT
Publishing Associate/FANFARE

FANFARE SPECIAL OFFER

Be one of the first 100 people to collect 6 FANFARE logos (marked "special offer") and send them in with the completed coupon below. We'll send the first 50 people an autographed copy of Fayrene Preston's THE SWANSEA DESTINY, on sale in September! The second 50 people will receive an autographed copy of Deborah Smith's MIRACLE, on sale in October!

The FANFARE logos you need to collect are in the back of LOVESWEPT books #498 through #503. There is one FANFARE logo in the back of each book.

For a chance to receive an autographed copy of THE SWANSEA DESTINY or MIRACLE, fill in the coupon below (no photocopies or facsimiles allowed), cut it out and send it along with the 6 logos to:

Here's my coupon and my 6 logos! If I am one of the first 50 people whose coupon you receive, please send me an autographed copy of THE SWANSEA DESTINY. If I am one of the second 50 people whose coupon you receive, please send me an autographed copy of MIRACLE.

Name _____

Address _____

City/State/Zip _____

Offer open only to residents of the United States, Puerto Rico and Canada. Void where prohibited, taxed or restricted. Allow 6-8 weeks after receipt of coupon for delivery. Bantam Books is not responsible for lost, incomplete or misdirected coupons. If your coupon and logos are not among the first 100 received, we will not be able to send you an autographed copy of either MIRACLE or THE SWANSEA DESTINY. Offer expires September 30, 1991.

Bantam Books SW 9 - 10/91 FANFARE special offer cut on dotted line

A man and a woman who couldn't have been more different — all it took to bring them together was a...

Miracle
by
Deborah Smith

An unforgettable story of love and the collision of two worlds. From a shanty in the Georgia hills to a television studio in L.A., from the heat and dust of Africa to glittering Paris nights -- with warm, humorous, passionate characters, MIRACLE weaves a spell in which love may be improbable but never impossible.

ON SALE IN OCTOBER 1991

The long-awaited prequel to the "SwanSea Place"
LOVESWEPT series.

The SwanSea Destiny

by Fayrene Preston

Socialite Arabella Linden was a flamboyant as she was beautiful. When she walked into the ballroom at SwanSea Place leading two snow-white peacocks, Jake Deverell knew the woman was worthy prey. . . . And at the stroke of midnight as the twenties roared into the new year 1929, Jake set out to capture the lovely Arabella, and quickly found he was no longer a man on the prowl — but a man ensnared.

ON SALE IN SEPTEMBER 1991
